What Gina C. Peabody Discovers in The Nutcracker

Andrew Carroll

"Splat!"

"Oh god, I've fallen again!"

Falling is but one of the challenges facing young ballerina Gina C. Peabody. Just staying vertical is a primary goal she hopes for to secure a good part in this year's production of The Nutcracker her school is presenting. Other technical feats will also test her determination in a year when four lucky dancers will be chosen from the show for a New York scholarship. But these are just the beginning of trials she will face: what roles she receives, will she be a contender for the prize, will her reluctant father agree to New York if she gets it, how does she navigate a sudden alliance with the school's nemesis and what that means for her friends who don't understand, and lastly, how to talk to her school crush. But most importantly, how will she stay vertical?! So much at stake! Seen through the eyes of Gina, the beauty of The Nutcracker unfolds with unexpected events in *What Gina C. Peabody Discovers In The Nutcracker.*

This novel is entirely a work of fiction. Any resemblance to actual persons, living or dead, is entirely coincidental.
Published by CompletelyNovel,com 2019.
Copyright @ Andrew Carroll 2019
All rights reserved. No part of this publication may be reproduced, stored in a retrieval system, or transmitted, in any form or by any means, electronic, mechanical, photocopying, recording or otherwise, without the prior permission of the publishers.
ISBN# 9781787233751

Special thanks to Mary Kole , who kindly advised me with honest and necessary editing and revision suggestions, and to all the dancers I have met, worked with, and become lasting friends with along my journeys. Lastly, a special thank you to my family near and far for their support and love, especially the real "Peabodys, including Gena," whose colorful home filled with humor and warmth served as the backdrop and inspiration for this project.

What Gina C. Peabody Discovers in The Nutcracker

A Novel

Andrew Carroll

Chapter One

Gina C. Peabody dashed out in the middle of class. Charlotte Tuddledum, her best friend, followed her out.

"Are you okay?" Lottie asked.

"Yes, I need water. That was a really tiring barre!" Gina said, referring to the first part of their ballet class.

"I know" Lottie replied, "your face is so red!" Gina looked into the mirror next to the water fountain to check; her face looked like a big cherry.

"Well, you know how I sweat" Gina replied,

"You sure do" Lottie said smiling, letting Gina know she wasn't making fun of her.

"At least we'll be ready for the audition" Gina added.

Gina took sips of water in big splashy gulps. When Lottie took her turn, she realized that they had been friends since they first began studying ballet at their school, The Ballet Academy.

"Gosh, that was eight years ago" Gina thought while Lottie continued to guzzle water.

"Lottie, we've been here since we were four" Gina said as Lottie finally stood up from the fountain.

"I know" she replied, wiping her chin.

The two dancers were very different in looks and in the way that they moved. Gina had long legs like a giraffe, blond hair and green eyes. Her very straight hair seemed to float perfectly into the bun hairdo. Gina's younger brother Benny always said it looked like Gina had a hamburger bun attached to the top of her head, an idea that usually made Gina hungry. Gina was gangly, a little accident prone, and often couldn't control falling out of turns. She wanted so badly to dance beautifully in romantic slow movements, and to look graceful in everything she did. She loved ballet, but it was a challenge.

Compact, spunky and always ready to burst into a round of giggles, Lottie Tuddeldum had very dark wavy hair that was oh so difficult to get into a bun on top of her head. Lottie had to use a lot of pins to get all those locks into place, and then a lot of hairspray to get it down nice and neat. This was not always accomplished well as their teacher, Miss Angelica, was often heard to shout out "Charlotte Tuddeldum…get those loose ends of hair out of your face!"

"You look as red as a tomato already, and we still have the second part of class" Lottie said, looking at Gina's face.

"You're right" Gina agreed. "I'll look like an alien when we finish at this rate."

Both girls squealed as Gina made a face back in the mirror, only making both friends laugh even harder.

Suddenly, Gina and Lottie's moment of fun was interrupted by Miss Angelica, who was ready to begin the center, or second part of the ballet class.

"Miss Peabody and Miss Tuddeldum, are you planning on coming back anytime soon?"

Both girls snapped around to see their teacher standing in the doorway with her hands on her hips.

"Ladies, we sip water when needed and return immediately. I would think that as twelve- year- old serious students, you would know that by now. We still have work in order to be prepared for the audition."

Under the watchful eye of Miss Angelica, Gina and Lottie silently and quickly scampered back into the ballet studio. Gina wondered if Miss Angelica secretly was hard of hearing because she often yelled out instructions.

Maybe she has sat too close to the music all these years, Gina thought.

Angelica Wentworth had been a well-known ballet dancer for many years with The National Ballet Company in New York City. Occasionally, The National Ballet Company toured to other cities, and in fact, they were scheduled to perform the holiday ballet The Nutcracker right in Gina's hometown right before Miss Angelica's production of it went up. Later, two of their biggest stars, Rosalie Bright and Logan Stark, were scheduled to perform the lead roles of the Sugar Plum Fairy and her Cavalier in Miss Angelica's show. The students already knew this and were excited not only about seeing a famous company, but getting the possible chance to meet Rosalie and Logan. But Miss Angelica also had a secret, one which she was planning on telling them later today.

Today's Saturday's audition was scheduled right after class. Miss Angelica's assistants, Miss Monica Monopoly (who had been a ballerina in England) and Mr. Andrew Black (who taught modern and jazz) would probably be helping out today to choose dancers for the different roles. Gina wondered whether either Miss Angelica or Mr. Black would be running her portions of the audition; Miss Monopoly was strict, and sometimes yelled at the dancers.

Gina secretly hoped that this year she would get to dance as a Snowflake in Act I and a flower in the Waltz of the Flowers in Act II. These were parts that required skill, artistry and most importantly, dancing on pointe.

Gina and Lottie rejoined the rest of their classmates who mostly smiled at the two friends when they took their places in the room. Gina got along with everyone, well, almost everyone. There was one crabby dancer, Viola Barkus, who frowned as Gina and Lottie assembled themselves. Viola seemed always sullen or annoyed. Her grimace now was just one of many that she usually made during the day. She also somehow always got the best parts. This was always confusing to Gina, because though Viola was actually talented and skilled, she didn't seem to ever want to work hard, and always looked unhappy in class. In addition, Viola usually sat silent in the dressing room and didn't talk to anyone.

"Ugh...the audition's today" Viola had said earlier in the day, almost out of the side of her mouth. Gina silently observed this peculiar way of talking, and secretly wondered if Viola was training to become some sort of performer in a mouth circus.

She always seems to speak from the side of her mouth, sort of like a snake might.

Gina remembered this as she peeked over to see if Viola was still frowning. She wasn't. Gina and Lottie often wondered why she was taking ballet in the first place. She wasn't interested in the movements or in the other dancers...why was she there?

As she and Lottie took their places, a red head slid in line next to them.

"Did we miss anything Viv?" Gina asked.

"No" whispered Viv, "Miss Angelica was waiting on the both of you."

Gina let out a breath of air in relief, and nodded a silent acknowledgment to Viv.

Vivica Snapple was smart. Not just smart, but really smart. She was usually the first one to show any moves to Miss Angelica because she was ready before anyone else was. Whenever someone was confused with any sequence of steps, Viv would demonstrate the phrase for them so they got it. Gina and Lottie admired Viv and chose to hang out with her as much as possible. The three of them went to the same school, ate lunch together and spent all their free time talking. Usually the conversations revolved around ballet, or Viola, or even about Ben and Bill Boxer, twin boys who also were in their class. The goofy Boxers were tap dancers, and wanted to tap on Broadway someday. Though they didn't necessarily like ballet, they were told that all Broadway dancers needed to know and be able to do it.

As Miss Angelica began showing the first center combination, Gina and the others watched her demonstrate the movements. Gina saw that the sequence would include a few tricky balances, ones that she sometimes stumbled out of.

Oh gosh, please don't let me fall out of those, Gina silently prayed.

As she began to go over the steps her focus was interrupted by Miss Angelica suddenly shouting "Boxer boys...do not, I repeat, DO NOT attempt to do a summersault in this, or any dance room unless the teacher asks for it!"

Gina noticed Miss Angelica scowling looking through the mirror backwards towards the side of the room. Sure enough, Ben and Bill were on the floor about to go over on their heads.

"Honesty" replied Miss Angelica, "You boys need to concentrate more on the dance steps instead of clowning around."

Gina watched as Ben and Bill slowing got up and sheepishly took their places back into the formation of their group.

Gina refocused on the combination Miss Angelica had just set and was struck by a realization: these particular steps were the same as the steps that the flowers did in the Waltz of the Flowers. "Maybe we're already being auditioned" Gina silently thought. Gina suddenly panicked thinking about those pesky balances and hoped they would not influence Miss Angelica's casting choices later. As if to confirm her thoughts, suddenly the door of the dance studio opened, and in walked Mr. Black and Miss Monopoly who usually did not visit Miss Angelica's class. They sat down in the front of the room and nodded to Miss Angelica.

Gina's heart started to race, and in that instant, she became nervous.

It *IS* some kind of audition she wildly thought. Taking a deep breath, Gina looked over at Lottie and Viv who also seemed to have figured out what was going on.

"Don't worry, you'll be beautiful" Lottie silently mouthed to Gina.

"What if I trip?" Gina pleadingly mouthed back.

"You'll be fine, just listen to the music and let your body take over" Lottie whispered.

Gina weakly smiled back at her, and then looked over at Viv who winked at her.

Then there was no more time to think as Miss Angelica announced "Alright, let's have the first group please." She turned the music on and Gina and the rest of dancers began.

Chapter Two

Sitting in a clump in the hallway after class, Gina and her two friends went over every detail of the combinations Miss Angelica set in front of Mr. Black and Miss Monopoly.

"Thank god I didn't fall out of my balances, well most of them" Gina said. "I wish I hadn't stumbled out of the first one though" she added. "I hope Mr. Black and Miss Monopoly didn't notice."

"I'm sure they didn't" Lottie replied. "It was the first thing we did, and they sort of were looking over at everyone. Besides, we were just getting started."

"Even if they did, by the time we got to the big jumps, I'm sure they hardly remembered as they watched you in all your glory" Viv chimed in. "And, if I'm not mistaken, that particular sequence of jumps is exactly the same as the ones done by whoever dances the Dew Drop" she finished.

It was true: Gina loved jumps or allegro, as it's known in the ballet world. She did feel especially happy being able to soar across the room effortlessly in the air. Miss Angelica often had her demonstrate; this sometimes made up for the falls she occasionally made elsewhere. Gina had always been thrilled to see other dancers cover space and look so free in the air, including the Dew Drop fairy part in the Waltz of the Flowers. All the flower parts were amazing, but the part of the Dew Drop really stood out.

"The Dew Drop part would be incredible to dance" Gina fantasized.

There was a sudden commotion as Hattie, Miss Angelica's secretary, emerged from the row of offices down the hallway with papers in her hands.

"That must be the lists of who gets to audition for what!" Gina squeaked out. All three jumped up quickly to join a huge mob of other dancers who realized the exact same thing. The large group clumped together at the bulletin board where Hattie was trying to post the papers.

Looking at the board, the girls saw they were listed as they hoped: each would be in the snowflake audition, "that's in 5 minutes" Gina murmured, and then each would also be in the coveted Waltz of the Flowers audition.

"We should get to the studio to get our pointe shoes on, what room are we in?" Lottie asked. Looking back at the board, Gina saw that both auditions would be in Studio C upstairs.

"Studio C…let's go!"

Walking into the studio they quickly began the process of putting on their pointe shoes. For Gina and her friends, this was a labor of love that came with a price: for years, all three girls couldn't wait until their feet were strong enough to begin learning to dance on pointe, yet, this often resulted in a lot of pain. Pulling out band-aids and fluffy lamb's wool, each girl began to quickly pad and protect their toes from developing blisters and bruises from being crammed into the small end of a pointe shoe and rising up on their toes in this small space. "I've got to get more lamb's wool, mine is almost falling apart" Lottie said. Miss Angelica always told them "You will get used to the blisters eventually, and you won't notice them at all when the curtain goes up and you are on stage." Gina questioned this at times, especially now as her toes already felt miserably squashed and the audition hadn't even started yet.

Once each girl finished, they began expertly tying the ribbons attached to the shoes around their ankles in a precise fashion. Miss Angelica had taught them that professional dancers always tie and secure their ribbons tight around their ankles, so that the feet have a clean line without hanging or loose ribbons to distract the audience. Each student at The Ballet Academy was drilled to look neat at all times, a true test of discipline for any young student. Standing up, each began warming up their feet in the pointe shoes by slowly rising up and down, allowing the feet to get used to being in this "torture chamber" as Gina sometimes called them when she could feel the blisters beginning to arrive.

As their feet began to get used to the shoes, Gina looked around to see who else was included for the snowflake audition.

"Almost all of our class is here" Gina out loud.

"Yes" Lottie replied, "Seems like we're almost all here, but then, it's a big group section."

Gazing around, Viv spotted Viola.

"Viola's also here" she said to Gina and Lottie. "Watch and see," Viv continued, "she'll be in the Flower audition too." Before Gina or Lottie could comment, Miss Angelica floated into the room followed by Mr. Black and Miss Monopoly.

"Alright girls, please stand and find a place in the room. We'll be learning three short phrases for the snow scene today. I will show them to you, and then I'll give you time to ask questions, and a few minutes to practice them on your own." As the dancers stood up, she added "spread out to give yourselves room girls."

At her words, a huge feeling of excitement rippled through the room. "Good, we'll begin with the entrance combination of the snowflakes." With that said, Miss Angelica began to demonstrate a short 32 count phrase, which included waltzing in place and finishing with a pirouette, or turn.

"I would like to see you all try a double pirouette please" Miss Monopoly yelled out.

A sudden hush fell on the room, as all the girls focused on the phrase Miss Angelica began to demonstrate. Gina, Lottie and Viv had placed themselves front and center so that they could clearly see exactly what was being shown, and to have the best advantage to learn the combinations.

Luckily for the dancers, many of the steps were in fact the same ones that they had practiced earlier in class. After a few minutes, it was time to perform

"Alright girls, shall we divide into groups and give it a go?" Miss Angelica asked.

She then counted off girls into groups. Gina and Viv landed up in the first group, while Lottie was placed in group two along with Viola.

Gina took her place in the center of the room, and waited excitedly for the music to start. Miss Angelica made her way to the side of the room where the CD player was located, and reached to press the button almost as if in slow motion. Gina's muscles and nerves were at a high pitch as this was the moment when casting might be decided. As the music began, Gina became transformed. Her body seemed to lift with the start of the melody, and she began to float through the movements. Because she was so at ease, her face radiated the pure joy of dancing until her feet unexpectedly crossed and she stumbled right into the preparation for the ending turn.

"SPLAT!"

"Wait, what?" Gina's temporary bliss came to a crashing halt as she realized that she had just fallen on the floor. She quickly stood and faked a graceful ending.

"Thank you group one. Group two, you're up" Miss Angelica said.

As she made her way to the side of the room, Gina whispered to Lottie as they switched places "how bad was that fall?"

"Not that bad; it looked like maybe you sort of tripped getting into the preparation."

Lottie continued to take her place in the center of the room, and Gina felt disappointment like a heavy weight in her chest.

Why do I always trip? Did they see it? Will it ruin my chances of dancing in the Snow scene?

Gina replayed her trip over and over in her head while Lottie's group auditioned, and she was so wrapped up in her thoughts that she didn't hear Miss Angelica's next announcement.

"Psst…Gina come on, we're doing the phrase again" Viv said as she steered Gina towards the center of the room again. Half in a daze, Gina followed Viv back out. As she took her place, she glanced over at Mr. Black and Miss Monopoly to see if their faces registered anything pro or con her way. Waiting for the music to start again, Gina suddenly felt nervous and shaky thinking about that last turn about to come up again.

Pushing herself through the music, Gina arrived at the dreaded preparation timidly, but did not stumble. Her turn, though not as good as it could have been, finished vertically.

Gina looked back over at the trio of teachers watching, but they all looked indifferent. She didn't have any clue as to what they were thinking.

As she passed Lottie yet again, her friend gave her a thumbs up to let her know she did better that time. Gina waited on the side while group two repeated the phrase, still anxious because of her first blunder. Seeing her worry, Viv slid over to stand next to her and said quietly "Gina, even if you stumbled once, you still always fill the room with such passion. Everyone sees it on your face whenever you do anything, even tripping!"

"Thanks Viv, I hope it doesn't cost me the part though."

Suddenly, the music was cut off, and Gina realized they were done with the phrase that Miss Angelica had given.

"Thank you, ladies, we'll have a short break, and then we'll begin the audition for the Waltz of the Flowers" Miss Angelica said as she went over to Mr. Black and Miss Monopoly. The three teachers then began a quiet pantomime in the corner, no doubt discussing how the dancers had done.

The Ballet Academy's version of Waltz of the Flowers had many different parts. Among them, the most prized one was that of the Dew Drop fairy, which had a special solo during the dance. Each year, the entire school waited in anticipation to see "who" got the part of the dew drop for that year. Usually, it went to the student who was one of the strongest, and who had good attendance as well as a good attitude. Gina, Lottie and Viv each secretly wished for this part. Each girl knew, however, that the school was large, and that there were many students who could qualify for this part.

As they were going into the hallway for water, Viola walked strongly over to Gina to cut her off from leaving the room.

"I bet you all want Dew Drop, good luck." With that, Viola walked out of the room ahead of Gina, leaving Gina wondering if she was being sincere or sarcastic.

Why would she even talk to me?

"Lottie, Viv, Viola just wished us luck for Dew Drop."

"Is she serious?" Lottie asked in surprise. "She probably sees you as competition."

"Competition?" Gina asked.

"Well, the solo has so many jumps, and you're good at them."

"Thanks, but a lot of dancers are good at jumps" Gina concluded.

"I hope anyone gets that part before she does" Viv said. "Come on, let's get water before the next round."

Twenty minutes later, the room was once again filled. As the girls waited, Miss Angelica strolled through the door talking with Miss Monopoly. The girls watched as Miss Angelica took a seat in the front of the mirrors, and realized Miss Monopoly would be teaching the flowers sections with Miss Angelica watching.

"Snip snap girls" Miss Monopoly tweeted. "Arrange yourselves about the room so we can begin." Gina and Lottie giggled at the sound of Miss Monopoly's high voice; she had some funny sayings which helped to soften her otherwise stern approach.

Soon Gina and the rest of the dancers were learning phrases that represented the different flowers in this section of the Nutcracker: the daffodil, tulip, daisy, petunia, carnation, violet, magnolia, orchid and of course, the dew drop. Though Gina was tired from the snow audition, her mind recognized that Miss Monopoly had made combinations that had sections from all the flowers in them. This way she and Miss Angelica could easily see who could do what. Gina made every attempt to look good in all the sections, to give herself a good chance at being cast in any role.

Diving into the choreography, Gina barely had time to notice Miss Monopoly and Miss Angelica whispering and pointing about the room, until Miss Monopoly's high squeaky voice shouted above the music "keep going dancers, and fill each movement with life!" With that, Gina threw every last bit of energy she had into her final set of steps, and was rewarded by glimpsing a smile from Miss Angelica who was suddenly watching her.

Finally, the music stopped and all eyes looked at the two teachers sitting in the front of the room, whispering yet again and writing the golden names on clipboards that they held in their laps. Gina would have given anything to see whose names were listed, but knew she would have to wait just like the others to see who was cast when the names would be posted on the bulletin board.

"Thank you, ladies, you all did wonderfully, and I would like to congratulate you all on all your hard work" Miss Angelica exclaimed as she stood to dismiss the students from the audition. "Miss Monopoly, Mr. Black and I will talk and we'll decide who will be cast in what parts in this year's production of our show. We'll post the names along with the rehearsal schedule when we're ready." With these final words, she smiled once more at the class and continued. "Please get dressed and come back to the studio. We would like to gather all of you together for a special announcement."

The hallway suddenly erupted in questions: "what's the announcement?"

"How did you do?"

"Wasn't that pirouette sequence hard?"

"Did you see them looking at you?"

"Who do you think will get Dew Drop?"

Gina, Lottie and Viv found their way to the dressing room, throwing sweat pants and sweat shirts over their black leotards and pink tights. They undid the ribbons of their pointe shoes, barely breathing as they recounted each moment of the audition.

"I'm still worried about that turn from the snowflake audition, but I'm more curious about what the announcement is" Gina said. Distracted by this thought, Gina sat for a moment staring in space trying to imagine what it might be.

"Come on Gina, we're ready to leave!" she heard Lottie say after a minute. Gina quickly grabbed her bag, not realizing her shoes were still on the bench beside her. She ran after Lottie and Viv who were already out the door, excited to find out what was in store.

Chapter Three

When the dancers reconvened in the studio, they saw that Miss Angelica was now not only joined by Miss Monopoly from the Flowers audition, but that Mr. Black and Hattie had also come in.

"Something big must have happened" Gina thought as she sat down and waited.

"Students, we have something very exciting to tell you" Miss Angelica said with a big grin, her head tilting up.

"As you know, The National Ballet is coming here to perform The Nutcracker right before our own production. In fact, I know many of your parents have already bought tickets to see this production. What you don't know, is that a week ago I received a call from their Director, Mr. Eric Stone, who had wonderful news: Mr. Stone is a personal friend of mine, and he has decided to stay here for a few days after they perform in order to attend our show. He will be watching all of you, and choosing four lucky dancers who will each receive an all paid expenses scholarship to study at their summer session in New York this next summer.

Gina immediately felt butterflies in her stomach.

A chance to study in New York!

Gina knew that New York was one of the leading places where ballet dancers lived and studied and it was her dream that one day she too might live there. She also knew of the National Ballet's famous summer sessions. World class teachers taught there, as well as many of their current leading dancers. Just walking in those hallways and studios would be an experience of a lifetime. It was usually an "audition only" process to get accepted to, and four of them would bypass that and be chosen in just a few short months.

But there are so many of us that are good...

Suddenly the bird-like voice of Miss Monopoly chirped "So it's VERY important that you all work as hard as possible in whatever role you're assigned."

"But we would expect that regardless; you must always work hard whether it's our production, or for any other production" Mr. Black added.

"Yes" Miss Monopoly agreed. "Hattie will post the cast list soon. We are always professional here, now we must be even more so. I will expect you to practice your given material on your own, and to not miss any rehearsals unless it's an emergency. We want to look extra polished when Mr. Stone arrives."

When she had finished, the room suddenly erupted into a buzz of multiple conversations. Gina thought all of it sounded too good to be true. She immediately wanted one of those four scholarships. All of it had so much promise, starting with the performance at The Grand Palace. Though she'd only been there a few times when her parents had taken her to see a few Broadway shows, she remembered it to be one of the most beautiful places she'd ever been in.

Gina thought about the first time she saw The Grand Palace going to see a musical. She recalled that when she first walked into the lobby of the theatre, she immediately felt like she was a glittering jewel in a case. Sparking chandeliers hung from the ceiling, catching light and spreading rainbows.

"Wow," Gina thought at the time, "I would love to perform here someday."

Gina remembered seeing people everywhere, each excited about the performance that was happening that night. Gina loved the energy she felt in this room.

Walking through this beautiful lobby, Gina entered into the actual theatre and was amazed at how much red was everywhere! Rich red velvet covered all the seats from one end of the room to the other. In the front, a giant red velvet curtain hung in over the stage looking like a giant cape that Red Riding Hood would wear.

It looks so soft; I would love to touch it, Gina had thought.

Later, she watched as the giant red curtain quietly lifted up to reveal a big stage filled with dancers, characters, scenery and lots and lots of movement under soft amber and rose-colored lights. Gina sat wide-eyed wondering what it would feel like standing under that warm light in a beautiful costume. Watching that show, Gina would always remember feeling like she was allowed access to a private fantasy world.

"Can you believe it?"

Gina snapped out of her theatre daydream to feel Lottie poking her.

"Can you BELIEVE IT?" Lottie said again.

Gina grinned, "I've never been to New York."

"Me neither" Lottie said.

Joining their conversation, Viv added "or me."

Before the girls could talk further, Viola interrupted to say "What's the big deal?"

"Big deal?" Viv said straight back. "Not only are we going to see a world-famous ballet company right here in our hometown, but four of us will get the chance at one of those scholarships… that's the big deal!"

"Well, to you guys maybe. It's just another reason for stress, and to have to get dressed up" Viola replied, as she bumped past the group to get her things and leave.

"What is with her?" Lottie asked watching Viola.

Gina also watched Viola leave puzzled as always by her behavior. It was one thing to be mean to her fellow classmates; maybe she was a bully. But to show no emotion over a really exciting opportunity was strange.

She must be unhappy about something in her life.

And for a moment, Gina felt sorry for Viola.

Focusing back on her friends, Gina said "never mind." We're going to the performance and some of us might go to New York! Besides, we'll also get to dress up, which opposite from Viola, I love."

"I'm going to go through my closet tonight" Lottie added.

"Me too" Viv said.

Gina gave a hug to both Lottie and Viv, and gathered up her bag. She suddenly realized that she couldn't wait to share the news with her family. She hoped that everyone would be as excited as she was; her dad Thomas did not always support her love of dance. Gina had to always explain that it wasn't a hobby for her, and that she wanted it to be her profession when she grew up. Thomas didn't see dancing as a real way to make a living, and usually reminded Gina that she would have to focus on more practical jobs eventually.

Maybe if I get one of the scholarships, he'll realize I have some talent.

Gina felt hopeful for a second as she made her way into the crowded lobby of the dance building to look for her Mom.

Chapter Four

Walking into the front of the ballet lobby, Gina immediately saw her mother, Alana Peabody, waiting to take her home.

"Mom!" cried Gina running over, "You won't believe what we just found out!"

"What?" Alana replied. "How was the audition?"

"It was good, I think; I fell out of a turn in class when everyone was watching, but other than that, I think I did okay. But wait, The National Ballet is going to pick four of us to study in New York next summer!"

"What do you mean?"

"The Director, Mr. Stone, is apparently a friend of Miss Angelicas' and he's coming to see our show! Then he's going to choose four dancers to study at their New York summer session, all paid for!"

"Which dancers?"

"I don't know, probably whoever dances well. It would be so amazing" gushed Gina, tripping as she made her way out.

"Well, I have some surprises too, but your news tops them" Alana said, catching Gina just as she was ready to fall.

"What's your surprise?" said Gina as she regained her balance.

"I'll tell you on the way home."

Gina ran fast to jump in their car and buckle up, waiting for Alana to tell her what the surprises were.

This is turning into an awesome day.

As Alana got in and made her way onto the road to take them home, Gina said "well?"

"Well" began Alana, "Lottie and Viv's moms and I got together when Miss Angelica told us about the ballet being performed here, and we decided we would make it an extra special night."

"How?"

"First, we are all meeting early at Papa Lou's."

"Papa Lou's, I love Papa Lou's!" Closing her eyes for a brief second, Gina thought about Papa Lou's, the best pizza restaurant in town. Gina, Lottie and Viv always begged their parents to take them there. Papa Lou himself was an old family friend who adored the Peabodys. Gina imagined his incredibly large pizzas, all glossy with pepperoni, sausage and lots of gooey cheese just dripping off on all sides. Gina's stomach suddenly growled at the thought.

"What's for dinner tonight?

"Chicken, mashed potatoes and salad" Alana said over her shoulder, as she made her way through traffic.

Gina loved this meal; she would always stab a piece of chicken and drag it through her pile of mashed potatoes.

Wow, I'm really hungry.

Gina was ready to look out the window for the rest of the ride home, when Alana continued.

"Wait, that's not all." She smiled as she snuck a peek back at Gina through the rearview mirror.

"It's not?" Gina asked.

"After the performance, we're going to go to Barnums."

Gina fell back on the backseat. Barnums was the most incredible and (in Gina's opinion) magnificent ice cream parlor in town. The front counter had jars of every colored kind of candy ever made; it was a rainbow of sweet heaven. There were so many choices it was hard to choose. Besides all the candy, there were ice cream sundaes, banana splits, and floats. Her favorite was a hot fudge sundae made with both vanilla and mint chocolate chip ice cream piled on a fudge brownie. She then had it topped with whipped cream and loaded with peanuts.

I wish we were there now.

"Since the performance is on a Friday night, after Barnums all the girls are coming over to our house for a sleep over. It's already arranged with all their mothers" Alana finished.

Gina and all her friends loved sleepovers. When the sleepovers happened at the Peabody house, sleeping bags and air mattresses were put out in the family room, ready for Gina, Lottie and Viv to burrow into while they giggled the night away. Often times, Gina's four- year -old brother Benjamin would run wild in-between all these impromptu sleeping arrangements.

"Is there any way Benny could do a sleep over that night somewhere else?"

Laughing, her Mom replied "No, he's still too little for a sleepover, but your Dad and I will make certain he leaves you and your friends alone."

"He always makes so much noise, and last time he popped Lottie's air mattress by jumping on it, remember?"

"Oh yes, I'd forgotten about that. Don't worry, he'll probably be asleep early."

"Okay" Gina said. "And could we also make sure Stella has a new chew toy to keep her busy as well?"

Stella, the Peabody's beloved golden doodle dog was as much a part of the family as any of them were. The problem with Stella was that she absolutely loved people…any people.

"Unless you get her a new chew toy, she'll be all over us all night, and she'll try to get into one of the sleeping bags with one of us again" Gina continued.

"Okay, I'll get her something to keep her busy as well" Alana said.

Gina picked up her bag to see if maybe there was some gum or any other snack to tide her over for the rest of the way home.

This feels light, something is missing.

"Mom, we have to go back!"

"What's wrong?"

"My pointe shoes; I must have left them at the studio."

"Oh Gina! How could you have left them. You know how expensive each pair is!"

"I know, I'm sorry! Dad probably won't buy me another pair!" Gina said with worry.

Frowning, Alana turned the car around and they began to drive back in silence.

"We haven't gone that far" Gina said meekly.

"I just hope your shoes are there, where did you leave them?"

"I must have left them in the dressing room, I had them on until then."

Alana was lucky to hit mostly green lights, and they shortly pulled back into the parking lot.

Walking back into the building, Gina was surprised at how quickly the building had cleared out.

Wow, everyone's gone. I'm glad the door is still unlocked.

Gina made her way down the hallway, and into the dressing room.

Oh, thank God, there they are.

Gina stumbled walking over to the bench where she had left the shoes, and stubbed her toe in the process.

Why am I always tripping?

She sat and rubbed her pinky in the silence of the room, willing her toe to stop throbbing. Finally, she stood and grabbed her shoes, and then was still for a second, eyebrows crinkling.

Something's wrong.

Though the building seemed to be deserted, she suddenly was aware that there were people still here, but it sounded like they were arguing.

She floated to the door as quietly as possible to try to figure out where the loud voices were coming from. After a moment, she realized they were coming from Miss Angelica's closed office. Coming out into the hallway, Gina was about to listen before she was startled by hearing Hattie who was standing in the other direction.

"Gina, what are you doing back here?"

Turning around, Gina said "I forgot my shoes and needed to get them."

"Well, I was just about to lock up" Hattie said, motioning towards the front door.

"Ok Hattie, have a good night."

Gina walked past her, and left the building.

"Did you find your shoes?" Alana asked.

"Yeah, but something weird was going on."

"What do you mean?"

"It looked like everyone was gone, but someone was having a fight in Miss Angelica's office."

"Who?"

"I don't know, it sounded like two women, and I think maybe I heard dew drop, but before I could get any closer, Hattie interrupted me. I wanted to try to listen and figure out who it was, but didn't get the chance to hear any more."

"Well, that is odd" Alana mused as she once again pulled out of the parking lot. "I don't know if I've ever heard anyone fighting at the studio."

"Me neither" Gina said, wondering who was behind those closed doors.

Chapter Five

The yellow Peabody home at 375 Magnolia Lane was surrounded by big oak trees with moss that hung from the many large branches. Their yard was full of flowers that seemed to bloom all year, and had butterflies that often flew back and forth between them. In the backyard, Gina had a special place: her Dad Thomas built a small one roomed treehouse into three huge branches of one of the oaks located in the corner of their backyard. This was Gina's favorite place to be.

Once you climbed up, there was a small door that you pushed open to crawl in. The room had special things:

An old carpet on the floor.

A stool.

Three shelves to hold books or Gina's favorite magazines, sunglasses, a radio and plastic forks and spoons.

A rope attached to a pail.

Gina especially liked the rope and pail. She'd often hauled up all sorts of treats to eat under the umbrella of the leaves. If the weather was nice, she and her friends would spend lots of time up there talking about all things secret.

Gina thought about the tree house as they walked in. It would be a good place to talk about the argument she heard. She plopped herself onto the couch making a mental note to call Lottie about this, but delayed her thought by asking "how soon is dinner?"

"Why don't you go and take a nice bubble bath while I finish making it" Alana said over her shoulder as she juggled pots, pans, and bowls.

"A very good idea" Gina agreed.

Gina loved bubble baths, especially right after a long dance class when her muscles felt tired and sore. She eagerly anticipated hearing the sound of the water filling the tub, and then pouring gobs of silky pink or gold bubble bath straight in. She loved seeing the soft puffy pillows started to form.

With that thought in her head, Gina made her way to the bathroom she shared with Benny, looking right and left, and then peeking into his room to make sure he was nowhere around to spoil her bath time.

Reaching into the cupboard by the sink, Gina looked at the bottles of bubble bath that stood there.

Will it be the gold lemony one, or the pink rosy one, she wondered.

Gina's arm reached for the pink bottle.

Roses tonight.

"Mmmmm, this will be wonderful right now" Gina said aloud to no one. As she started to put the bottle back into the cupboard, Gina suddenly heard a scratching noise at the door.

Please don't let it be Benny.

Opening the door just a wee crack, Gina saw the beloved golden doodle waiting outside the door wagging her tail.

"Oh, come on in Stella" Gina said opening the door wider.

Closing the door, she giggled as she watched Stella walk over to the rim of the tub and sniff the bubbles. The dog always got confused with bubbles. She would try to smell them, and then back away as they broke on her big brown nose.

"It's just bubbles Stella, you've smelled them before" Gina whispered to the dog while she petted her. As she rubbed her ear, Stella melted against Gina.

"Okay big girl, go lie down so I can get into this tub"

Stella must've sensed the petting was done for the moment because she stretched herself down to lie on the furry bathroom rug beside the tub. Gina tested the water with her hand, and then slipped into the mountains of bubbles.

Perfect.

As the warm water and bubbles began to ease her sore muscles, Gina allowed her mind to drift into the story of The Nutcracker:

The ballet begins at a Christmas party hosted by an elegant couple, The Stahlbaums. The scene on stage is a beautiful living room, where Dr. Stahlbaum and his wife are greeting guests who have arrived for a Christmas party. Appropriately, there is a well decorated Christmas tree at the center of the room, filled with candy canes, jeweled ornaments, sparkling lights, and festive ribbons. Amidst the arriving guests are the two Stahlbaum children, Clara and her younger brother Fritz, each excited for the upcoming festivities.

As the room fills with guests and their children, the party begins. Beautiful music and dancing mixes with the eager romping of the excited youngsters. Suddenly, at the height of the party, there is a hushed silence at the arrival of a mysterious new guest; a tall man with an eye patch carrying large boxes and gifts. Clara immediately recognizes him as her Uncle, Herr Drosselmeier, who is known to bring magic wherever he goes. Clara runs and hugs her beloved Uncle, and waits to see what is hidden within the large boxes he brought. As the room clears with anticipation, Herr Drosselmeier opens the first box and out jumps a life size ballerina doll. She is colorfully dressed in a pink and green tutu, and dances for the eager guests. When she finishes, she is placed back in her box, and another box is opened to reveal another life size doll: a soldier doll. He is dressed in blue and red, and carries a sword which he uses throughout his dance. Clara and the guests clap with delight when he is finished and also returned to his box. Clara thanks her Uncle, and in turn, he presents her with a gift: a Nutcracker doll.

Clara is enchanted with her new gift, but hardly has time to play with it as Fritz snatches it away from her and accidentally breaks it. Heartbroken, Clara clutches the broken doll, but is relieved when, through magic, Herr Drosselmeier fixes it and returns it to her.

After the party finishes and the guest go home, Clara wanders back into the party room alone, and lays down on the sofa. She dozes off, and is awakened by the chiming of the grandfather clock striking. Suddenly, as Clara gets up, the Christmas tree starts to twinkle and begins to grow, and grow before her eyes, until it is taller than it seems her house is. Dazzled by the beauty of it, Clara is taken by surprise as a giant mouse runs past her, and is followed by another, and yet another. Clara runs back to the sofa she fell asleep on, and soon is surrounded by an army of giant mice, running circles all around her. Frightened, Clara looks around at the scary mice that seem to lock her on the sofa she sits on.

As Clara stares unbelievingly at the towering mice, a giant life size toy soldier comes to fight the mice. He is soon joined by an army of other giant toy soldiers, who engage the mice in a battle. As the fight ensues, the King of the mice enters, to help his army to victory. However, Clara is stunned when she sees her Nutcracker doll, now also a grown live soldier, enter to fight the Mouse King to free Clara. They soon launch into a furious fight, and Clara, hoping to help, throws her slipper at the Mouse King. The slipper hits the Mouse King in the head, which distracts him long enough to enable the Nutcracker to kill him. With the death of their king, the rest of the mice surrender, and they exit carrying off their leader. As the battle is now finished, the toy soldiers also leave the stage.

Clara approaches the Nutcracker to thank him, and is surprised when her uncle, Herr Drosselmeier, appears and sits them in a beautiful white sleigh he has magically brought. As Clara and the Nutcracker sit down in the seat, it takes off and whisks them into a beautiful white winter forest where snowflakes appear and dance all around them welcoming them to their woods. Within this delightful landscape, A Snow King and Queen appear and dance for Clara and her Nutcracker, and then send them on their way to the magic kingdom of The Land of the Sweets.

"Fifteen minutes until dinner!" Alana's voice boomed from downstairs.

Gina's beautiful vision was temporarily broken by this summons, but she slid deeper into the water to continue her lovely trip through the rest of the ballet.

The second Act of the Nutcracker begins with Clara and the Nutcracker Prince arriving in The Land of the Sweets. Giant cupcakes, candy ribbons and sweets fill the delicious landscape. Little angels, dressed in long white dresses, come to welcome Clara and the Nutcracker Prince. They dance happily at their arrival, and are soon joined by the Queen of The Land of the Sweets, The Sugarplum Fairy. Clara looks adoringly at this *beautiful ruler; she is the most radiant woman Clara has ever seen. She is dressed in a rose and plum tutu, with tiny jeweled fruit and candy fixed to the material, and a sparkling tiara on top of her head. She smiles warmly at Clara and her Prince, and gestures for them to sit at a candy throne prepared just for them. Here they will sit and watch different dancers from many lands, all who have traveled to welcome them.*

As soon as they sit, music begins, and Spanish dancers with hot chocolate enter wearing rich brown velvet with ribbons of red encircling their costumes. Their dance is lively, and exciting.

Next, dancers from Arabia slowly slink in, carrying exotic coffee as a gift. They wear flowing silks in oranges and blues, and their dance is elastic and mysterious.

Just as soon as they leave, a giant box is rolled in, and out pops a dancer from China, dressed in a vibrant yellow and green kimono costume. He brings with him Chinese tea as a gift, and jumps thorough a series of high energy leaps before landing back into the box at the end.

As the box is wheeled off, a group of Russian candy cane dancers appear, dressed in stripes of pink and white. They, in turn, are followed by shepardeses from France, who bring candy marzipan to the festivities. They wear cream and turquoise tutus, and dance with flutes to call their sheep.

As they finish and bow to Clara and the Prince, the couple gape at the largest woman they have ever seen, Mother Ginger, who has come to greet the couple. As she stops in front of them, out scampers one of her children from underneath her skirt, then another, and yet another until 8 children are dancing in patterns across the stage dressed in green and salmon skirts and pants. Scampering back under their mother's dress, they bid the couple goodbye and leave Clara and the Prince who wave goodbye in return.

Beautiful waltz music next fills the stage as different flowers enter to dance surrounding a beautiful fairy in the middle of all of them; the Dewdrop Fairy. She is delicate and dressed in a small tutu of iridescent light blue-green, with sparkling raindrops in her hair. She dances in and out of the flowers in an exquisite waltz, weaving in and out of the blooms just as a drop of water would. She finishes this waltz glistening in the middle of all the flowers.

Saving the best for last, The Sugar Plum Fairy now enters with a handsome Cavalier, and they dance the most elegant pas de deux, or dance for two as it's known, for the couple. Clara sits hypnotized by the sheer beauty of this dance: by the beautiful tutu worn by the fairy queen, by the bejeweled tunic worn by the Cavalier, by the long lines of her legs as they lift and stretch with beautifully pointed feet, and by the way she seems to float in the air as she either rises on the tips of her toes across the stage, or is lifted high into the air by her male partner. As they finish their dance, all the other dancers join them in a finale, filling the stage with breathtaking color, movement and characters.

Clara is delighted with the party that has been presented in her honor, but realizes it's time to go home. The Sugar Plum Fairy guides her back into her sleigh, and she and the Prince fly off into the night back to her home, eagerly waving good-bye to the beautiful land that brought so much magic to the night.

Gina realized the water had started to become cold.

"Get up Stella" she said as she reached for a fuzzy towel to dry off.

Stella lifted her head for a second and then began to stretch her long legs.

"Gosh Stella, you would think you did all the dancing today from the way you're stretching!" Gina said down to her.

Even though Stella had no clue what Gina just said, she began to wag her long feathery tail back and forth.

Chapter Six

"In your pink robe and fluffy slippers, I see" Alana said as Gina walked into the kitchen. Gina arrived just in time to see Alana putting delicious smelling chicken and downy mashed potatoes on the table.

"Yum" Gina cried out eying the spread before her.

"I second that!" said Thomas as he walked into the kitchen as well.

"Hi Dad."

"Hi Gina."

"Do you know about all the plans for the night when we go to see The Nutcracker?"

"I do, your Mom told me."

"Gina had some exciting news today" Alana said, setting a salad next to the potatoes.

"What's the news?" Thomas asked.

"The Director of The National Ballet is coming to see our show to pick some of us to study in New York next summer" Gina said, wondering what her Dad would think.

"New York!" Thomas blurted out. "That sounds expensive."

"No" Gina continued, "whoever he chooses will get a scholarship and an all-expenses paid opportunity to study with the National Ballet" Gina said, hoping it might impress him.

Gina watched Thomas scratch his head about to say something, but stopping before any words came out. Gina guessed he would once again start talking about practicalities and work, or something that Gina didn't care about. He usually distrusted the dance world and thought that it was fine for now, but not for an actual career. He didn't get that all she would care about right now was getting one of those four slots, and to eventually being a professional dancer.

Gina watched her Dad look at Alana changing the subject to ask "where's Benny? It's unusually quiet in here."

Okay, at least he didn't say absolutely no to New York.

"Probably playing his new space video game that I bought him today" Alana said finishing tossing the salad.

"Does the space game have sequels?" Gina asked suspiciously.

"I think so, actually quite a few of them"

Maybe Mom or Dad can buy him more of this game for the sleepover night in case he's still up.

Satisfied with a possible Benny distraction for the sleepover, Gina turned her concentration on the dinner sitting on the table. Gina's mouth watered as she pulled out her chair.

"Thomas, go find Benny" Alana said serving the salad.

"Here we are" Thomas said dragging Benny into the kitchen, sitting him down.

Gina looked at her little brother who looked so much like her. Benny also had blonde hair and green eyes, and was actually cute, though Gina would be the last person to admit it.

"How was bullay?" Benny asked looking over at his big sister.

"It's 'ballet', not' bullay' Gina said, "and it was great."

"What made it great?"

"We had our audition for the Nutcracker, which is always exciting."

"You mean tryout?"

"Yes."

"Did you get in?"

"I don't know yet."

Gina changed the subject asking Alana "is the Barkus family also going to The Nutcracker?"

"I don't know" Alana replied, "Why?"

"Well, Viola always brings the mood down" Gina said, in-between mouthfuls of chicken and mashed potatoes.

"Well, it's a pretty big theater, so chances are she'll be somewhere far away" Thomas said.

"I hope so."

"Maybe you girls should try to be nice to her" Alana said, pushing Stella away from trying to snatch a piece of chicken from the table. "Maybe she just wants to be included."

"MOM" Gina almost shouted, "We are nice! It seems like she doesn't want anyone to include her."

"Sometimes people are misunderstood, and just need a little more time than others to fit in" Thomas weighed in.

"What's for dessert?" Benny asked.

"I bought a blackberry pie and we'll have it with some vanilla ice-cream in a bit" Alana said. "Why don't you go and get into your pajamas? By that time, I'll have it ready."

Benny loved dessert. This fact was not lost on Gina. While Benny ran off, she asked "Mom, is Benny also going to The Nutcracker, and Barnums?"

Laughing, Alana exclaimed "No, don't worry, we'll get a babysitter for that night so he can stay home. We know how he can be at Barnums."

Satisfied with that answer, Gina started to help carry the dishes to the counter, where Thomas was rinsing and putting them into the dishwasher. Stella, who'd run with Benny to his bedroom, was swiftly back to the kitchen. She no doubt realized that her last chance at getting anything from the table was winding down.

Gina heard Alana say "Here you go Stella," as she gave Stella a small piece of chicken. Stella literally gobbled it down in one second flat.

"Does she even taste it?" Gina asked, staring at Stella licking her muzzle.

"Who knows? She just likes to be included" Alana said over her shoulder as she began to cut the blackberry pie into slices.

"Dessert!" Alana yelled to Benny, who sprinted from his bedroom. Alana pulled the ice cream out of the freezer, and began rolling big scoops to put on top of the pie pieces.

Gina once again had to admit that Benny looked awfully cute sitting in his chair smiling for his dessert. But not cute enough to have him come to Barnums the night of The Nutcracker though. He turned wild looking at all the candy there.

All four Peabodys attacked the dessert, enjoying the flaky crust and globs of blackberries that mixed with the smooth vanilla ice cream.

"Thanks Mom, that was a really good dinner" Gina said when they'd all finished. Deciding to be bold, Gina asked "Dad, wouldn't it be amazing if I got one of the places for New York?"

"I'm not sure Gina. It sounds like a bit much for a twelve-year old."

"I'll be thirteen by next summer!"

"I don't know."

"Dad, a lot of thirteen-year-olds do these summer sessions."

"Gina, I said I don't know."

"Let's cross that bridge if you get even chosen" Alana broke in.

Gina wanted to continue in the hope that she could sway her Dad's mind, but knew that when it came to dance topics, sometimes it was smarter to back off for the time being. She looked at Thomas, who looked down at the empty plates in return.

Conversation's over.

Gina got up and made her way to her room, followed by Stella who'd apparently decided for whatever dog reason that Gina was the person to be with at that moment.

"Stella, I have no food, and I am just going to do homework" Gina said, looking down at the wagging tail and furry body. "But come on in anyway" she finished as she reached the door to her room.

Chapter Seven

Gina's room was lilac. All lilac. Gina loved this shade of purple, so it was everywhere.

Lilac bedspread.
Lilac pillows.
Lilac curtains.
Lilac walls.
Lilac chair.
A world of purple bliss.

Gina walked in and sat down on her bed knowing she should start her homework, but wanted to call Lottie or Viv instead.

Lottie and Viv need to hear what I heard.

Gina was about to pick up the phone, but got sidetracked thinking about what she might wear the night of the performance.

"It's going to be a big night, so I want to wear something special" she said aloud to Stella, who was finishing circling round and round on the lilac throw rug beside Gina's bed before curling up on it.

"Stella, you should come with me to ballet so they all could see just how perfect your circles are every time you get ready to lie down" she said to the dog. Then she expertly hopped over her furry body, beelining to her closet door.

Pulling open the door, Gina began to look at the row of dresses hanging like a parade of clothing.

Hmm, let's see.

Gina's hand first went to a sunny yellow dress that had pretty blue and green embroidery at the collar and at the waist.

"I love this dress" she murmured as she swept it off the hanger to take over to the full-length mirror hanging on the wall. Holding it up to herself, Gina realized that it looked more like something she would wear in the spring or summer months, not this colder time of year.

"Okay, back you go" she reluctantly said.

Well, if it's holiday time, then maybe I should be wearing something red or...green! as her eyes settled on a deep green velvet dress with a black sash that tied around the waist.

Gina whooshed the dress over to the mirror and smiled as she knew that this was the one.

Just as she was putting away the green dress her phone rang. As she reached for it, she saw that it was Lottie.

"Hi Lottie, I was just about to call you."

"Did your Mom tell you about everything we're doing the night of The Nutcracker? And are you hoping to get the chance to go to New York as much as I am?"

"Yes, and yes. My Dad wasn't thrilled about New York. Even if I do get a shot, I don't know if he will let me go. But wait, I have to tell you about what I heard."

"What do you mean, what did you hear?"

"I forgot my pointe shoes at the studio, so we went back to get them. When I got there, I heard what seemed like two women having an argument from inside Miss Angelica's office. I couldn't hear what they were fighting about, but I did hear one of them say dew drop! What do you think that means?"

"I don't know! Who was in the office?"

"Before I could find out, Hattie stopped me in the hallway and sort of made me leave."

"Wow, have you told Viv?"

"No, I was about to call both of you, but went through my clothes to pick something out."

"Let me guess, the yellow dress?"

"No, it doesn't fit with the holiday time, so I decided on that dark green velvet dress I have."

"The one with the black sash?"

"Yes."

"That looks great on you."

"Thanks, what about you?"

"I think the pale blue dress that I wear with that white sweater."

Gina knew that dress and sweater, and had always thought that Lottie looked pretty in it.

"Good choice."

"Thanks, call Viv and tell her about what you heard."

"I will."

"Okay, I need to start on my homework" Lottie finished.

"Me too" Gina said.

Hanging up the phone Gina was about to call Viv, but reluctantly reached over to her backpack to pull out her homework. She again thought about Thomas's stubbornness towards anything related to ballet. Gina was surprised that he even was going to go to both of the Nutcrackers. The nagging thought crept up again.

What if I get chosen and he doesn't let me go?

Deciding to call Viv later, Gina gave Stella a quick pat on her head and settled down to concentrate on her assignments.

Chapter Eight

Walking down the school hallway the following Monday, Gina was preoccupied thinking about the casting that might be posted that day. Spotting Lottie down the hall, Gina broke into a faster walk so she could talk before the homeroom bell rang.

"Lottie" Gina spoke out.

"Gina!"

"I've been looking for you since I got here, do you think the casting will be up when we get to the studio this afternoon?"

"I hope so, did you talk to Viv after we talked on Saturday?"

"I filled her in yesterday. She doesn't know anything either."

Spying the red hair coming down the hallway, Gina and Lottie went to meet Viv who looked impatient with the crowded hallway.

"Hi guys," Viv said in her usual dry voice.

"We were wondering if the casting will be up later" Gina said.

"I know, I hope it is" Viv said swatting people out of her way.

As the homeroom warning bell rang out, the three quickly said goodbye to begin their day.

Gina was a smart girl and was in all advanced classes for her age. She was challenged by devoting time to both her studies and dance training, but knew each was important. Because of this, she sometimes missed out on regular school functions and wished she had more friends beyond those at ballet. Her time was so limited that she could not participate in most school functions such as clubs and dances. This made her feel like an outsider at times. But dance was too important to give up. She knew this in her heart. Still, she would have liked to have more of a social life at school.

After homeroom announcements were wrapped, Gina picked up her bookbag to make her way to math, her least favorite class. Gina often thought that the only "math" that she enjoyed was adding pirouette numbers to her turns, or subtracting mistakes from choreography. She questioned why she needed to even study math. Mr. Proctus, her strict math teacher, thought otherwise. He threw complicated fraction problems, story problems and other assorted math puzzles constantly to his students. Gina often found herself working more on math homework than on any other subject.

"Good morning students" Mr. Proclus almost shouted, as if the volume of his voice could force interest into the subject.

Gina hoped she could keep her mind off of the Nutcracker, and forced herself to pay attention. As her day progressed, Gina looked forward to lunch. Just before, however, she walked to her second least favorite class, Phys Ed, with Miss Shouldersgirth. Since Gina was a dancer, she was in excellent condition. She wondered why it was necessary for her to swing a bat or throw a ball for forty minutes with Miss Shouldersgirth barking somewhere in the distance "FASTER!, HIGHER!, MORE MORE MORE!" She danced for at least two hours every day, and put forth more effort in one hour of dance than in all the gym classes combined. However, it was required at her school, so Gina gamely smiled and waited to see what activity they would be doing today. Luckily, it was an obstacle course: running, climbing a rope (for a very brief instant), diving under a bar, jumping over hurdles, more running, and finally leaping over a mat to finish. Years of ballet training had made Gina very coordinated, so this task should be a breeze today. As Miss Shouldersgirth yapped out the instructions, Gina made her way to the front so she could get the exercise over with.

"YOU READY PEABODY?" Miss Shouldersgirth shrieked at Gina.

"Yes."

Please don't let me fall.

Suddenly the strong gym teacher blew what had to be the shrillest whistle invented, and Gina was off. Gina's strong legs from ballet quickly ran to the rope, and she grasped the end and rapidly pulled herself up to the required height. She released herself on a diagonal so that she could swing into the bar, gracefully diving under the pole. Next, she got to the hurdles, and imagined that she was doing pas de chats, or the "cat" step in ballet, where you have to pick up both legs one after the other in a jump. This made the hurdles a snap to accomplish; the height of her jumps easily clearing the several obstacles. Gina eyed the finish mat in the distance to leap over, and sprinted towards it and flawlessly lifted herself into a huge grande jete, or split leap. She sailed over the mat with plenty of room left over.

"WELL DONE PEABODY!"

Happy that she was finished, Gina walked over to the side of the gymnasium and sat down.

Wow, I didn't stumble or trip. Why can't I manage that in ballet?

Gina sat by herself and began to watch the others pairing up and laughing as their social circles were connected.

I wish Lottie and Viv where in my gym class, then at least I would have people to talk to.

But her friends were on different schedules, so Gina would have to wait until lunch when she could reunite with them. Fortunately, it was the next period up, and it looked like the obstacle course was just winding up. In fact, Miss Shouldersgirth was roaring commands at the last student, who apparently was going much slower than she wanted.

Mercifully, the bell finally rang for lunch. Gina ran to her locker, grabbed her lunch, and then went to the lunchroom to find her friends.

Seeing Lottie and Viv, Gina sat down with them at their usual lunch table.

"It's an obstacle course in gym today" Gina said in-between bites of her sandwich. "Running, a rope, hurdles and jumping over a mat."

"I can manage that" Lottie said.

"Maybe Shouldersgirth might actually smile for once if I can sail over the mat" Viv added.

Deep into their conversation, Gina heard a sudden "Hi Gina!" Turning, she saw one of her classmates, Jake Preston, wave at her.

"Hi Jake."

Jake was one of the popular boys at school, and smiled as he walked past to join his friends at a nearby table.

"That boy likes you for sure" Lottie said.

"Yep, and he's not only good looking, he's one of the nice ones too" Viv said.

Gina blushed, and waved her hand as in whatever, but she looked back at Jake. She admired his curly brown hair and brown eyes, as well as the fact that he was a good student. Because his little sister Amanda studied ballet at Gina's school, he had seen many of the productions that Gina had performed in. He always made it a point to find Gina after any show to tell her how well she had done. Everyone at school knew Jake had a crush on Gina. What everyone didn't know, though, was that Gina had a crush on Jake as well.

"Something catch your eye?"

Gina recognized the voice, and steeled herself.

"Hi Viola."

"Jake likes you."

Turning around to the voice behind her, Gina said "He likes everyone."

"Yes, but…never mind."

Gina looked eye to eye with Viola for a moment, not understanding why she had chosen to even speak to her. Viola in turn looked at Gina, and broke the momentary silence by asking "Think the casting will be up later today?"

"I hope so" said Gina, not trusting this sudden conversation, or its source.

"Yeah" was the only reply from Viola, who turned around as quickly as she had appeared, only to disappear back into the crowded lunchroom.

"What was that about?" Lottie asked.

"I don't know" Gina said.

"Suspicious" Viv added.

"I agree" Lottie finished.

Gina briefly caught sight of Viola across the room talking and laughing with a group of other girls. It occurred to Gina that Viola was actually popular with other girls here at school, and seemed to blend in nicely. She looked happy here. Gina took in her long smooth brown hair and pale blue eyes and had to admit that Viola was pretty. Unfortunately, at ballet, her constant bad mood overshadowed her other features.

Why is she so different here?

"Gina?"

Looking at Lottie, Gina realized she had just asked her something.

"What?"

"Where were you?"

"Sorry."

"I said Viola is just weird."

Gina just shrugged her shoulders in response.

Chapter Nine

Arriving at the Ballet Academy, it seemed that every student had the same thought: impatient students bolted out of barely stopped vehicles see whether those sheets of paper listing the roles had been pinned up. Alana had hardly put their car into "park" before Gina was out the door.

Breathless, Gina made her way into the crowded hallway where the bulletin board hung. She saw to her dismay that there was a crowd already 3 people thick surrounding the board.

I'll just have to worm my way in there.

Squeezing herself through any possible opening, Gina wove through until she was standing smack in front of the board.

It's up!

Gina quickly scanned the headings of the parts until she spied the "Snowflake" listing and ran her eyes down the names listed.

Gina C. Peabody!

Gina's heart sped up for a second taking in this information. Continuing on, Gina quickly found the Flowers listing to look at those names.

Gina C. Peabody- Tulip.

TULIP! *Wait, that's the smallest part. Everyone knows whoever dances Tulip has "problems."*

Gina backed out of the mob to organize her thoughts about being given this role.

Why Tulip? I know I can handle a bigger challenge. Maybe I'm not that good.

Gina realized that she wanted to know who got the other parts, specifically her best friends. Gina threaded her way back to the board to look.

Going back to the Snowflakes listing, Gina saw that Lottie and Viv would also dancing in that section. Lottie was also cast in the Flowers section, in the role of the Carnation.

That's a great part. I need to be happy for her.

Looking for Viv's name, Gina saw that she was only listed as an understudy for some of the flowers.

At least I'm cast. I hope she's not upset.

As she was turning to go find her friends, Gina's eyes caught the words "Dew Drop" on the casting list, and Gina's mouth flew open.

Viola Barkus.

Viola?

Why would she be awarded the part of the Dew Drop?

Viola did in fact have technique Gina had to admit. But the part needed attention, determination and most of all, passion to look professional. Viola definitely did not have passion. She always complained and acted like she would rather be anywhere else. Gina was so baffled by this that it took her a moment to see the writing right below Viola's name.

(Peabody to understudy Dew Drop.)

Wait...what?

This was one of Gina's most beloved parts of the ballet. The Dew Drop had the most dynamic choreography that darted with surprise through the flowers. The pale blue green tutu for the role was (in Gina's opinion) the most beautiful of all. It was studded with rhinestones so it made whomever wore it sparkle through each pattern of movement.

Viola is going to wear that costume.

It didn't seem fair. Then it hit Gina that not only was Viola going to get this opportunity, but that Gina would have to be in the same room with her rehearsal after rehearsal watching from the sidelines. It felt like a window shade lowering on any excitement she had felt moments ago.

Gina left the board and wanted to find someplace to be alone for a moment. She rounded the corner leading towards the dressing rooms, and almost collided with Lottie who was anxious to find her.

"Gina!"

"Hi."

"Have you seen the casting?"

"I did."

"Gina...you're learning Dew Drop!"

"I know, but under Viola."

"Yeah, but still, it's a lead part!"

"But I'm only the understudy, and my actual part is Tulip, and we all know what that means."

Gina saw Lottie looking desperate at her.

"What?" Gina finally asked, in reference to Lottie's expression.

"Gina, you're a beautiful dancer because you have that amazing body and you seem to be filled with so much joy in every step you take. You literally glow when you move."

"But?"

"Tulip doesn't have any tricky turns in it, and you know how nervous you get when there's a turn involved."

Gina felt hot tears looming: Lottie was not saying anything Gina didn't already know. To hear them voiced was just validation.

"Gina, someday you'll outgrow tripping when you figure out why you stumble or understand your body better and get stronger so you won't fall as much. But until then, you will still shine in anything, even the tulip."

"Thanks Lottie, it's just crazy that Viola got Dew Drop."

"I know, her attitude's a bummer. But skill wise, she can handle the part if she just puts some energy and life into her face."

"I'm going to have to stand in the back as a runner up watching her dance one of my favorite parts" Gina finished.

Gina abruptly realized Viv was not with them.

"Has Viv seen the casting?" Gina asked quietly.

"Yes, she has" said Lottie. "She got here before I did, and already knew when I saw her."

"Is she okay?" said Gina.

"Actually, she is. When Viv got here, Miss Angelica saw her and called her into the office. She told Viv that she was a beautiful dancer, but that she had another role that she needed Viv to learn; the Head Angel."

"Oh, I didn't even look at that part when I looked at the casting."

Gina thought about this for a moment, and then realized what a perfect part this was for Viv. The Head Angel greets Clara and her Nutcracker Prince when they arrive in the Land of the Sweets at the beginning of Act II of the ballet. The role is responsible for leading a group of very young dancers representing angels who are also there to greet Clara and her Prince. Since these angels are sometimes scared, they need someone to watch and help them along for what was usually their first experience on stage. The Head Angel role always was assigned to someone who learned choreography quickly, and who could learn the parts of the younger dancers and lead them in case they forgot once they got on stage.

"Perfect for Viv" Gina exclaimed.

"Yes," Lottie continued, "and she is still understudying the Flowers section as well."

"Just like me with Dew Drop. Lottie, do you think everyone's going to think I'm not good because I got the Tulip part?"

'Gina, you're also the understudy for Dew Drop. That's a major part. Any one of us would be thrilled if we were considered at all for that role. Viola will probably perform it, but if for some reason she couldn't, then I don't think Miss Angelica or the others would take the risk of putting just anyone as the understudy. They see something in you. Everyone does."

"Thanks Lottie. Oh, and Carnation is a great part for you."

"Thanks. Let's go find Viv."

Seeing the mane of red hair in the back of the dressing room, Gina motioned to Lottie to follow her.

"Viv" Gina said catching her friend's attention, "you're going to be an awesome Head Angel."

"I know, I'm glad, I really like that part and I'm excited to open Act II." "So, understudy for Dew Drop eh?"

"Yeah, but Viola?"

"I know, go figure, maybe that's what the argument you heard was about."

In her worry about her own casting, Gina hadn't thought of this yet. Her eyebrows narrowed suspiciously.

Oh, that's interesting.

"We better get to the studio; our class is in a few minutes" Lottie reminded them.

Gina looked over at Viv and whispered "I wish you were a flower."

"I'm okay with it, really I am."

Gina put her arm around Viv feeling slightly better about the casting, and the three left the dressing room to get to class. They soon were engrossed in talking, and failed to see a lone person hidden way in a dark corner of the hallway. Sitting on the floor, Viola Barkus was silently crying and hoping no one would see her.

Chapter Ten

Gina wandered into the kitchen six weeks later on a Saturday morning, and promptly ran into the side of the wall.
"OUCH!"
Turning from the counter Alana cried out "What happened?"
"I just stubbed my toe!"
"Oh Gina, you have to be more careful!" Alana said placing a plate of crisp buttered waffles down in front of Gina. "Maple syrup, or raspberry jam on top?"
"Syrup" Gina said, inspecting her toe.
Alana opened up the bottle of syrup and poured zigzags all over the top of the waffles which were just about to travel on their way to Gina's fork.
"Delicious" Gina mumbled taking a bite.
"How are rehearsals going?" Alana asked as she poured some juice.
"Not as bad as the first few weeks, at least I'm not as sore anymore. Dew Drop is still awkward."
"Still?" Alana said as she sat down with a cup of coffee.
"Yeah, it's confusing. Not the choreography, but Viola."
Gina had both eagerly anticipated and dreaded the start of rehearsals. So far snowflakes rehearsals had been hard because there were so many patterns which shifted pretty quickly like a real snowstorm. Gina's challenge was to remain on balance when she needed to change her weight on pointe to move in a new direction; she had (gasp) fallen many times already. At one point, Miss Monopoly had been thinking of taking her out of the section, until Miss Angelica had stepped in to reassure her that Gina just needed more time to adjust to the fast choreography. The process had made Gina insecure as she seemed to be the only one falling.
One night after a particularly shaky rehearsal, Miss Angelica told Gina to come see her in her office when she was done changing back into street clothes.
"Oh god, they're finally taking me out of Snowflakes" Gina thought as she numbly put her jeans and sweatshirt on in the

dressing room. Her body felt empty with the dread that she could lose her part and dignity all in the same moment.

Why am I so clumsy?

Gina knocked on the door.

"Come in" Miss Angelica's voice rang out.

Gina turned the knob with a sweaty palm and walked in.

"Sit down Gina."

A suffocating bubble of anxiety filled Gina's body, and she sat down almost ready to cry.

"I've noticed that you are having some problems in rehearsals, and I wanted to talk to you about them."

Gina sat quietly, wanting to respond somehow, but empty of words in her fear.

"Gina relax; I want to offer some help to get you stronger."

"Are you taking me out of the part?" Gina almost whispered.

"No, no." Miss Angelica pulled a chair out to sit next to Gina. Taking her hand, she said "you're a lovely dancer, such passion and lush phrasing, …but… you need some help with those long limbs of yours and weak ankles, all which betray you."

Standing up, Gina watched as Miss Angelica opened a drawer and took out a long green piece of wide elastic.

"This is a theraband, and I want to give you some exercises with it that might strengthen your feet and legs to work with better assurance and efficiency" she said.

Gina felt the vise of doom beginning to leech out of her body.

"Theraband?" she said back in a voice so meek it might have come from a new born kitten; apparently all the doom still had some ways to go exiting her body.

"Yes, it's a terrific tool to strengthen your body, just watch some of these exercises."

Gina sat and watched as Miss Angelica expertly wove the elastic looking long scarf around the bottom of her feet, and began alternately pointing and flexing her feet against the resistance of the material.

"It's hard in the beginning, but once you get the hang of it, you'll want to do this every day to get your feet stronger" Miss Angelica said with a slight whoosh of voice that matched the rhythmic pulling she was doing with her feet. Gina saw that her jaw was slightly clenched as she focused on manipulating the band while she said this.

It must be hard; her face looks so...concentrated.

Miss Angelica rattled off what seemed to be dozens of these flexes and pointes, and then yanked the band off her feet with a big smile, satisfied with whatever small workout she had just demonstrated.

Is her upper lip sweating?

"Here, you give it a try."

Gina took the theraband and wrapped it under her feet just as Miss Angelica had. She began to flex and pointe and thought "hey, this isn't so bad at all."

Miss Angelica stopped her after a mere few seconds.

"Pull hard on the band" she said.

"What?"

"Gina, pull as hard as you can with both hands on the ends of the band, so that it's hard to flex and pointe."

Gina pulled on the bands as hard as she could, and then found it really difficult to pointe her foot.

With her head tilting sideways with a nod, Miss Angelica replied "exactly." "You want to make it hard so that your feet get used to pushing which will make them stronger."

Gina tried it a few times this way, and soon felt a trickle of sweat fall down her spine in reaction. She also felt as if her calf muscle had just run a triathlon.

"This is hard!"

"It is Gina, but if you have discipline, and dedicate some time each day for this, you'll see improvement in how you are able to keep stable."

Gina tried a few more times, until she felt like her leg would certainly edge into a massive cramp. Miss Angelica nodded again, and silently walked over and gently took the band back. Within a minute, she was showing Gina more exercises for other parts of her body.

Gina watched grateful for all these tips, but daunted by the volume of work this conditioning represented.

When am I going to have time to do all of this?

When Miss Angelica had finished, Gina thanked her and started to put the band into her bag.

"If we can get you stronger, you will be a force to reckon with" Miss Angelica said as Gina gathered up her things.

Chapter Eleven

As Gina ate her waffles that Saturday morning, she thought about how much she hated doing the theraband exercises, but had to admit that she actually hadn't fallen so much lately. In fact, she also was not as sore as she had been, and her ankles seemed to be holding her up better.

"Why is Viola confusing?" Alana asked as Gina swirled her waffle bits into a sea of syrup.

Gina's eyebrows creased as she took a gulp of orange juice thinking about her first Dew Drop rehearsal alone in the room with Viola. Miss Monopoly was in charge of the Dew Drop section (to Gina's dismay; Miss Angelica was nicer), so there were only three people in the room, two of which were not favorable to Gina.

At first, it almost didn't matter: Gina felt invisible in the room. Viola, well Viola usually ignored her, and Miss Monopoly seemed only interested in coaching Viola. Thus, so far, Gina had stood in the back, memorizing the steps and trying valiantly to plug along with no one seemingly caring whether she was there or not. Then, out of the blue, Miss Monopoly got frustrated with Viola not remembering the sequence of steps one night, and left the two girls alone as she exited the studio "to have a moment." Alone in the silence, Gina boldly offered a suggestion to Viola's stumbling block by telling her to keep stepping in the direction she is landing in from a jump, rather than stopping from the jump, to lead her into the next sequence logically. Viola's stopping was somehow breaking the pattern in her head, and she needed those extra steps to continue the phrase.

Viola had not sneered, snarled, insulted, barked or any one of her usual reactions, but rather, had looked at Gina, and then turned herself around and repeated the phrase with the additional two steps to guide her into remembering the choreography and... it worked.

Though she did not thank Gina, she none-the-less had also not ignored her at best, or said anything awful at worst. The only validation Gina got back was Viola's next statement, said to no one in particular.

"That works."

When Miss Monopoly came back, she glared once at Viola and said "I certainly hope you have the choreography by now" as she made her way back to the sound system to put the music back on.

Apparently, her "moment" included some type of crackers as Gina noted crumbs on the old tattered sweater she always wore at night.

Viola robotically took her place in the center of the room, and actually returned Miss Monopoly's glare as the music began. As the trouble spot loomed, Miss Monopoly's finger inched its way towards the stop button in anticipation that Viola would falter, but Viola took the extra steps that Gina had suggested and continued through to the next phrases.

Viola finished the rest of the material they had learned and stopped to face Miss Monopoly.

"Well, I'm pleased that you must have figured out how to remember the steps" Miss Monopoly said with extremely squinted eyes. Gina questioned her sincerity: "was that a compliment?"

Viola said nothing, not even a reference that Gina had, in fact, helped her.

"Why do I care if she gives me credit?" Gina thought.

Because I would have if it were reversed.

Then, to everyone's surprise, Miss Monopoly said "Okay, Gina, let's have a look at you."

Viola slowly turned her head to look at Gina, and backed away towards the side of the room to allow Gina to take the center.

Oh my God.

Gina meekly walked into the center to take the starting position of the Dew drop solo.

Why do my legs feel shaky and weak when they felt fine a minute ago? What happened to all that Theraband work?

Miss Monopoly pressed "play."

Gina began the steps, and though she knew the choreography, she repeatedly fell out of any turns that occurred.

After her third fall, Miss Monopoly stopped the music and yelled "Gina, you're going to have to get stronger to get through this part if needed!"

Gina felt humiliated, and wanted to cry, but managed to keep her head up somehow.

"That's enough for today ladies, I suggest you both think about what this part means to any serious dancer, and apply the work needed to be successful" Miss Monopoly said like a ballet dictator. She then lifted her chin to look at each of them for a moment, and then turned off the sound system and left the room without a goodbye.

Gina felt defeated, and began to gather up her things.

"Your back foot."

Gina turned around, surprised.

"What?"

"Your back foot is not planted on the floor to take off evenly. It's not connected to the floor like your front foot is. That's why you are falling out of the turns" Viola said generically.

Gina stared at Viola, at first not registering that she had even spoken to her, let alone taken some interest in giving her any kind of tip.

Without speaking, Gina walked back into the center of the room to take the position needed for a turn. Viola did not move, but watched as Gina placed her feet in preparation.

"Watch the way your back foot rests on the floor. You never get it firmly on the ground in order to have an even foundation to take off from. If you can feel your little toe on the floor, then you've placed it evenly and you will have more stability for your turn that comes out if it" Viola stated flatly.

Gina incredulously took another instant to comprehend that Viola was possibly offering her help. She then concentrated to feel her back foot, and realized that she naturally placed her back foot on the ground favoring her big toe, which meant that the bottom of her foot was not a flat surface to take off from.

Gina forcibly put her foot down flat and took off for a turn.

She rose effortlessly into a beautifully executed turn and landed into a solidly clean position that even Monopoly would complement.

Without saying a word, Viola gathered up her belongings and left the studio.

"Gina! I asked why is Viola confusing?" Alana repeated to Gina who had momentarily stopped eating.

Alana's question brought Gina back to the Saturday morning breakfast.

"I'm not sure, but I think she actually may have tried to help me."

"Really?"

Gina leaned forward on the kitchen table and verbalized the events that had just played through her mind.

When she finished, she looked to Alana for some kind of explanation as to Viola's out of character tip.

Unfortunately, all Alana could offer was "hmm' with a diagonal tilt of her head, standing to take the empty plate away.

Chapter Twelve

Gina finished her breakfast and trotted back to her room to put her hair up in a bun. Pulling it back first into a ponytail, Gina began to circle it around and around on top of her head while putting bobby pins in to secure the hair in place.

"There" she said as she finished and looked at herself in the mirror.

Good enough.

"GINA C. PEABODY LET'S GO!" shouted Alana who was waiting by the front door ready to take Gina to ballet.

"Coming!"

Gina closed the door to her room, and ran to the front door.

Leaving the house, Gina saw their kindly neighbor, Bea Bumble pulling up the last of the weeds in her garden.

"I'm gonna getcha out" Miss Bea screamed at a weed she frantically was tugging at. Gina watched as she pulled once, pulled twice and then "BAM!" Out came the weed with such force that Miss Bea fell on her behind.

Gina giggled and yelled out "hi Miss Bea!"

"Well hello Gina" she replied back, waving a plump and dirty hand at Gina.

Gina giggled even more as Miss Bea wiped her forehead with her hand, dragging a large dirt streak across her face.

"Going to ballet class?"

"Yes Miss Bea."

"I heard you have some special events coming up."

"Yes, we're going to The Nutcracker next Friday, and then our own opens the week after."

Miss Bea smiled. "I'll be watching your younger brother those nights."

"Oh, that's perfect, Benny loves when you babysit him."

Bea Bumble loved the Peabody children. Since her own children were grown and had moved away, she enjoyed to watch Gina and Benny. Once, when Miss Bea had watched Gina, Lottie and Viv together when their parents had all gone out to dinner, Miss Bea had asked them to help her make a cake, and then frost it. The girls had loved this as she let them lick the different spoons she used. Later, in Gina's bedroom, Viv said absentmindedly "you know, if you reverse her name, it's funny!"

Gina and Lottie staring blankly at Viv not knowing what she was talking about.

Miss Bea Bumble…if you reverse it, it becomes Bumble Bea."

It took a moment for this to settle in on both Gina and Lottie, and then suddenly they both smiled.

"BUMBLEBEE!"

In all the years that Miss Bea had lived next door, Gina somehow had never thought of putting that together.

Gina remembered this as she looked at Miss Bea's smiling dirty face. She ran over to give her a hug and said "Have a good day Miss Bea!"

"You too honey, have a good class today."

Waving goodbye, Miss Bea turned her attention back to her garden, and soon Gina heard her once again yelling at another poor weed.

Gina and Alana got into their car, and pulled out of the driveway. As they were driving away, Gina looked back at the house and saw Stella's face watching them from a window.

"Mom, what do you think Stella does all day when we're away? Gina asked, seeing the last of Stella's head at the window disappear.

"I'm sure she sleeps, walks around, who knows?"

"Or maybe she sits and tries to figure out how to open the refrigerator door once everyone's gone."

Alana giggled. "Perhaps."

Gina smiled imagining that image, and then changed gears.

"Have you and Dad talked any more about New York?"

"Not yet, but I'll try to bring it up again soon."

"Why doesn't he get it?"

"Gina, he does, in a way. Of course he wants you to be happy. He just hasn't grown up with ballet in his life the way you have. He wants you to be successful and stable later in life, and thinks a career in ballet won't give you those things."

"But it makes me happy."

Alana sat silent for a moment. "He isn't educated in the value of passion. We'll have to find a way to get this across to him."

Gina thought about how this might be accomplished, but couldn't think of anything at the moment. Instead, she asked "can Viv and Lottie still come over today after class and rehearsals?"

"Sure, what are you thinking to do?"

"We haven't had any time to just chill lately. Maybe we'll go up in the treehouse, we haven't done that in a while."

"In the treehouse?" Alana asked with hesitation, "isn't it getting too cold?"

"If it is, then we'll come inside."

Looking out the window, Gina thought about the times she and her friends had spent in the treehouse. In its perch, it was the perfect place to laugh, share secrets and talk about anything privately. Going up there seemed much more appealing at the moment than the thought of class and rehearsal. As much as she liked dance, Gina was hungry for some fun as well.

When they pulled up to The Ballet Academy, Gina reluctantly slid out of the car to go in. As she made her way in the door, she almost bumped right into Jake, who was standing just inside the door.

"Hi Gina."

"Oh, hi Jake, what are you doing here?"

Please let my face not turn red. Why did I put on these ratty sweatpants?

"We're waiting for Amanda. Her class is just finishing."

He is so handsome.

"Is she excited to perform her first Nutcracker?"

Laughing, Jake answered "that's all she talks about."

Standing so close to Jake, Gina couldn't think of anything more to say. Her mind struggled to find something of interest.

I'm so lame!

"There she is now" was all she could come up with as she gestured at Amanda making her way into the lobby.

"Are you ready for your own performances?" Jake asked waving Amanda over.

"Getting there, still a lot of rehearsals left to go" Gina replied, fumbling to find some kind of witty conversation to keep Jake intrigued.

"I'm sure you'll be fantastic as usual" Jake replied as he took Amanda's hand to lead her out.

"Bye Jake."

"Bye Gina."

Gina watched them leave, and then wished she had taken a little more time to look more presentable.

And why can't I JUST TALK around him?

Chapter Thirteen

Once inside, she found Lottie and Viv already in the studio waiting for her.

"Hi Gina" Lottie said.

'Hi."

"What's wrong?"

"Nothing. I don't feel like working all day."

And I wish I had been more interesting to Jake.

"Neither do we. Are we still on to come over later?"

"Yeah. Maybe we can go up to the treehouse if it's not too cold."

"That would be fun."

Before Gina could add anything more, a voice behind her said "one day the floor of that wobbly treehouse will break and you'll all fall down to the ground."

Turning her head, Gina looked straight at Viola who had appeared out of nowhere.

"What do you three do up there?"

"What do you care?" Viv asked.

"I don't, it just seems weird" Viola said back.

"It's not, but you'll never get it" Viv continued.

"You're right about that" Viola finished as she brushed past.

"I can't imagine your Dew Drop rehearsals with her" Lottie said, frowning at the back of Viola.

"Let's just get through this day" Gina said, not convincingly.

And let me not fall out of my turns.

And let Jake be interested in me.

Gina took a deep breath to clear her head just as Miss Angelica entered the room.

"Good morning students."

"Good morning Miss Angelica" they replied.

"Are we ready for the performance coming up next Friday?" she asked the class.

The whole room nodded.

Miss Angelica smiled, and then suddenly stopped when her eyes fell on a frowning Viola.

"Is there something wrong Viola?"

Caught off guard, Viola replied "no."

Gina noticed that Miss Angelica's face almost looked sad for a moment, before turning to start the class.

Once class had begun, Gina unusually lost focus. She continued to think about Jake, her turns, the treehouse and everything but the class material. Out of the blue, the music stopped.

"Gina, you don't know the combination."

Gina froze as she realized Miss Angelica was looking straight at her, and so was everyone else.

Gina was mortified that she was so lost in thought that she was blank as to what steps Miss Angelica had just given that everyone else (even Viola!) were currently doing. She was a model student...this never happened to her.

"Well?" Miss Angelica asked putting her hands on her hips.

"I'm sorry."

"I suggest you get organized Gina. We are in the final days before our own performances. And may I remind you, remind everyone" she exclaimed louder, eyes scanning the room "that four of you will have the chance to be awarded those scholarships based on how well you dance. I would think that at this point all of you would be in high gear to excel."

With these last few words, her eyes finished their virtual scan and landed squarely on Gina.

Gina felt humiliated. She had never been called out by Miss Angelica for any wrongdoing. Even though no one in particular was looking at her any longer, she felt like the whole world had a magnifying glass on her. She dared to glance over at Lottie, who looked as upset for Gina as Gina was herself. This made Gina feel even more engulfed with shame, and she wanted to burst out crying. It was surreal to fall back into class as though nothing had just happened.

When class finished, Miss Angelica motioned Gina over.

"Where is your head today?"

"I'm sorry...I don't know."

Seeing Gina's panic, the hard lines of Miss Angelica's worried face softened.

"Gina, it's not like you to be so unprepared, so unfocused."

Gina had nothing to say back. She felt her whole body folding in, like Stella when being scolded for eating a shoe.

Putting her hands on Gina's shoulders, Miss Angelica said in a gentle voice "Gina, I think you have so much talent and promise, and I would be so sad if you didn't live up to the exciting potential you have. I remember being your age, and having moments when the ice of discipline would crack just a bit. I was able to push through, and was rewarded with a career that I am so very thankful to have achieved. I see that same kind of work ethic and drive in you, and hope you are able to continue to climb towards a beautiful career in ballet as well."

Gina knew her eyes were watering, but she kept her emotions in check and nodded faintly back.

"Now go off to rehearsal, what do you have right now?"

"Dew Drop."

"Collect your thoughts and energy, and have a good rehearsal."

Like that's possible at this point.

Gina grabbed her bag, and started walking down the hallway towards her rehearsal studio.

"Gina!"

"Oh Lottie, I'm so embarrassed" Gina almost cried meeting Lottie halfway down the hall.

"Are you okay?"

"Yeah, no...I mean I just got lost in thinking about things. I've never been lectured in class before."

"You should see me in math class at school" Lottie joked.

Gina stood still for a moment, and then smiled at Lottie's attempt to make her feel better.

"Thanks Lottie."

"No sweat Gina; it always feels worse than it actually is."

"Was everyone talking about it?"

"No."

"Okay. Really?"

"Really."

"I have Dew Drop now; I'll see you later in Flowers rehearsal."

"Have a good one."

"Thanks Lottie."

Gina walked into the studio to find Viola already in there, expecting to hear her say something about class. But instead, Viola only looked over as the door opened, and then went back to getting her pointe shoes on.

"Ladies, let me grab the music and then we'll begin" Miss Monopoly shouted as she breezed into the room out of breath. Turning to Gina, she said as an afterthought "and I hope you are focused now. I heard you are having some concentration issues today. We'll start with you today."

Great. Did Miss Angelica tell everyone?

Gina dumped her things onto the floor and mechanically began to get her shoes on, wondering if somehow Miss Monopoly was going to make rehearsal difficult for her today.

"You always know the combinations. Miss Angelica shouldn't have made such a big deal the one time you didn't."

Gina stopped tying her ribbons and looked up. Viola wasn't looking at Gina, but rather, was tying on a ballet skirt in which to rehearse in.

"For what it's worth, I think she was trying to get everyone on edge because of the shows coming up, and used you as a scapegoat" she finished as she tied a tight knot on her skirt.

"I actually didn't know the combination" Gina said hesitantly, not knowing how to navigate this sudden conversation with Viola.

"You're allowed every now and then, why does the world revolve around ballet?" Viola asked, finally looking Gina directly in the eye.

For a moment, the two pairs of eyes locked. Gina felt like this was somehow a tipping point of…what?

Viola wants to say something.

"Alright ladies, let's begin" Miss Monopoly's voice commanded as she walked back into the studio, interrupting the unexpected turn of events.

Gina watched as Viola's focus withdrew from Gina, and became neutral with Miss Monopoly's arrival.

"Miss Peabody, you're up" Miss Monopoly declared, with just a hint of malice.

Gina stood and walked to the center of the room to take her place. Preoccupied with all that she had encountered this day, she slipped into automatic mode and once again placed her foot incorrectly for the first set of turns in the variation.

She fell out of the turns.

"STOP!"

Miss Monopoly's hand victoriously flew to the stop button of the music, and turned to face Gina.

"Miss Peabody, we are less than 2 weeks away from the performances. Even as the understudy, it is curious that you haven't worked on fixing your turns this close to the shows. This is unprofessional."

"AGAIN!"

Gina walked back into the center, and saw Viola rubbing the bottom of her foot out of the corner of her eye. She was not sure if Viola was trying to give her a cue about putting her whole foot on the floor, or was just coincidentally rubbing her foot. When the music led up to that point once again, she firmly pressed her foot down and spun around expertly and landed ever so gracefully into a perfect finish. This shocked Miss Monopoly, who had begun to trace her hand automatically back to the stop button.

As the music continued, Gina fed all her frustration and emotion into the solo. The room disappeared, and only music and movement existed. Somehow, her exasperation about today's events hammered the need to place her foot correctly throughout the solo. When she finished the variation, there was silence in the room.

"Well...that was better" Miss Monopoly offered meagerly.

Gina stood in the middle of the room, and felt *different*.

Looking through the mirror, she caught Viola smiling, but it didn't look like a smirk. Viola's lips were turned upward, not downward in what was her usual lip placement. Catching Gina's recognition equally in the mirror, Viola's face instantly changed; not bad, not good, but just became her usual neutral.

Looking then at Miss Monopoly, Gina stood and waited for any comments or corrections, which usually came after she ran through the part. Miss Monopoly seemed to be at a loss for words. Again, Gina felt

different.

I've never felt so powerful in my dancing. It's as though I stopped thinking, and just let my body MOVE. It was so exciting.

In what seemed like an hour, but in reality, was just a few seconds, Gina had found some courage in tackling her dance challenges.

Maybe those theraband exercises helped after all. And Viola's help.

Miss Monopoly broke the silence by turning to the music and saying over her shoulder "Viola?"

Gina walked over to the side, and watched Viola gloriously sail through the variation, despite having no expression on her face. Gina had to admit that Viola danced that variation beautifully, though it would be enhanced if she just matched her face to her stellar skills.

"Very good Viola" Miss Monopoly stated. "That's enough for today ladies, please keep this energy up for the remainder the rehearsals we have left." With that said, Miss Monopoly began to gather her things, as did Viola who, without a glance this way or that, focused on getting her belongings and leaving the room.

Gina also turned, expecting something: a complimentary response from Miss Monopoly? Some kind of kinship with Viola?

Both left the room without any further word, leaving Gina standing alone in the studio.

I want one of the New York spots.

Chapter Fourteen

After the group Flowers rehearsal, which mercifully went uneventful, Gina found Alana in the lobby waiting to take her home.

"Hi Gina."

"Hi" Gina replied almost muted.

"What's wrong?"

"It was a weird day; I'll tell you later. Lottie and Viv can still come over, right?"

"Yes, their Moms are picking them up in a few hours."

As Gina waited for her friends to finish getting dressed, she saw Viola's Mom Patricia enter the lobby with a bright pink coat in hand right next to them.

For a moment Gina looked quizzical.

I'm missing something.

"Hello Alana."

"Hi Patricia."

"That's a beautiful color of pink" Alana said, admiring the coat.

"Viola rushed out today without it, and it's definitely colder out now. Hi Gina, how are your rehearsals going? Viola tells me you're her understudy for Dew Drop."

Gina again looked hard at Miss Patricia. "They're hard, but going well" was all she could sum up still looking hard at...*what?*

"Well, I'm sure you are just as excited as Viola for the shows, and to be considered for the New York summer scholarship. I think it's a great opportunity; we're all hoping Viola gets one of the slots" she finished smiling at Gina.

Before anyone could reply, Lottie and Viv showed up, followed by Viola.

"Hi Miss Alana."

"Hi girls, ready? If you all want to spend some time up in that treehouse, then we need to get home before it starts getting even colder."

"Can we just go?" Gina almost pleaded.

"Is everything okay?"

"Mom, I'll tell you later" Gina whispered harshly.

Alana looked worriedly back at Gina.

"I'll tell you in the car" Gina softened, sensing Alana's concern.

As they passed by Viola, Gina waved a small goodbye.

Viola looked away.

Looking towards the door, the three friends watched Viola in her pink coat leave with her mom. Alana followed them through the open door.

"There's something about Miss Patricia" Gina said to Lottie and Viv as she started out.

"You mean if she had brown hair she would look like Miss Angelica?" Viv answered.

Gina looked quickly across the pavement and saw Viola and Miss Patricia getting into their car. Miss Patricia's blond head disappeared quickly into the cavity of their car.

"She DOES look like Miss Angelica; I don't know why I've never made that connection" Gina said, startled by the revelation.

"I've always thought that" Lottie concurred.

As they reached the car, Gina's thoughts were interrupted by Alana asking "what happened today Gina?"

Scrambling into the car, Gina replied in-between adjusting herself into her seat belt "Miss Angelica called me out for not knowing a combination."

"What do you mean?" Alana asked starting the motor and pulling out. "Why didn't you know it?"

"I don't know. I was just thinking about a lot of things and got lost in my thoughts. I mean, it's not like I do it every day."

"Maybe Jake had something to do with it" Viv said, reaching across to jab Gina playfully in her side.

"No, it wasn't Jake, or maybe it was a little bit" Gina admitted, pushing Viv's hand away.

"Did you see Jake today?" Alana asked weaving the car into the main road.

"Yes."

For a moment, no one said anything; a clue that Jake did indeed have more to do with it than Gina would admit.

Lottie broke the awkward silence, saving Gina by saying "Gina, you're allowed to make a mistake in class every now and then. I do it all the time."

"How did it end?" Alana asked worriedly.

"Miss Angelica talked to me after class. She was nice, but I was embarrassed."

Gina stared ahead, hoping the conversation revolving around her day would stop. She saw Alana glancing at her through the rear-view mirror, and looked away lest she continue asking questions.

Turning into their street, Alana changed the direction of the conversation saying "I'll make a quick lunch for the three of you. Grilled cheese?"

"Great" Gina replied, relieved that the subject had been changed. The mood of the car seemed to lift as they pulled into the driveway.

Chapter Fifteen

After lunch, they scrambled out to the yard, eager to climb the ladder up to their beloved space.

"Oh, I'll miss this place until it gets warm enough next spring when we can come back up here" Gina said as she entered into the nook nestled in the oak tree.

"Me too" Lottie added, emerging head first followed by Viv.

"We've had some fun times up here."

Crawling in, the three girls arranged themselves in the cramped quarters. Gina reached over and hauled up some brownies she had put into the bucket below. Putting them in the middle, each took one and bit into the layers of chocolate. Silence ruled as they savored the taste for a moment.

"Gina, how much do you like Jake?" Viv asked swallowing her last bite.

Caught off guard, Gina hesitated for a second, and then decided to tell the truth.

"He makes me so nervous every time I see him; he's so handsome."

"I agree" Lottie said licking her fingers. "The handsome part that is, he doesn't make me nervous."

"When I saw him this morning, I couldn't think of any good things to say. That always happens any time he starts to talk to me. He must think I'm really uninteresting" Gina lamented.

"If that's the case, then why does he always try to talk to you?" Viv countered.

"Maybe he's just trying to be nice" Gina offered.

"I don't think so, no one's that nice" Viv said back.

"I bet his family is going to the Nutcracker performance" Lottie said. "Maybe if you plan ahead in your head, you can rehearse some things to talk about."

"Lottie, that seems…unnatural or something" Gina said frowning. But after a moment of thinking, she added "but maybe you're right."

"Are there any more brownies?" Lottie asked absently.

"Yeah Gina, they taste almost as good as the ones at Barnums" Viv added.

"Barnums!" Lottie cried out hugging herself. "I could live there!"

"Papa Lou's is pretty good too" Gina added, suddenly thinking about the plans laid out for that night. "We deserve to go to both of them after all these rehearsals."

"How did Dew Drop go today after class?" Viv asked randomly.

"Why do you ask?" Gina answered

"Well, class was so…rough for you today. I was just wondering because you had that rehearsal right after the Miss Angelica thing. And…I would have hated to have had to be in a studio with Viola right after that. She probably gloated because you got yelled at."

"Actually, she sort of stood up for me in a way" Gina replied.

"What?"

"Right before rehearsal began, she told me that she didn't think it was right of Miss Angelica to call me out."

"Viola?" Viv pressed on.

"Yes, Viola Viv."

"You're talking about Viola Barkus, correct?"

"Viv, we only know one Viola" Gina said leaning in towards her friend.

Gina looked at Viv and sensed some kind of challenge rising, and saw Lottie shift uncomfortably as a confirmation of her thoughts.

"I know it sounds weird, but Viola has been different in the last few sessions we've had together" Gina said cautiously.

Gina expected Viv (or Lottie) to say something, but both friends just stared at her.

"She DID stand up for me today, and the other day she gave me a tip for landing my turns that really helped" Gina continued, wary by their silence.

"Gina, I can't believe you are supporting Viola, and even taking tips from her" Viv said a little louder than her normal voice. "How can you trust anything that comes out of her mouth?"

"Her tip worked Viv" Gina said evenly. "You would have to be in those rehearsals with Miss Monopoly yelling right and left to understand."

"Oh, yes, I'm not good enough to be the *UNDERSTUDY* for Dew Drop" Viv said sarcastically.

"Viv, that's not what I'm saying at all!"

Gina was confused by this turn of events. Before either could say anything more, they all heard a

"SNAP."

"What was that?" asked Lottie.

"Ugh, probably Benny, let me see" Gina said as she got up to look over the side of the treehouse.

Peering down, Gina didn't see Benny, in fact, she didn't see anyone.

"There's no one there." Gina said turning back to the center of the treehouse.

"Viv, I'm just saying…"

"SNAP." Another noise, but further away.

Lottie and Viv stood to look over the side with Gina, and then Viv said all of the sudden "over there!"

Gina and Lottie turned to look in the direction of where Viv was pointing and saw a pink coat disappearing into the tall bushes leading out of the Peabody's yard.

"Viola!' Gina said in wonder.

"Viola?" Lottie asked in wonder as well.

"That's definitely her coat" Gina declared.

"Why would Viola be here?' Lottie asked.

"Well, she does live nearby" Viv replied

"Do you think she heard us?" asked Gina.

"Who cares?" Viv answered annoyed, turning to face Gina. "Don't worry, you didn't say anything bad about your new best friend."

"Viv, she's not my new best friend! What's wrong with you?"

"What's wrong with me?! What's wrong with you Gina? It's always been us against Viola."

"Viv, she's just been different lately is all I'm saying. I'm not saying she's my new best friend, you are!"

"Girls, you need to come in soon. Lottie and Viv's Moms are on their way to pick them up" Alana's voice yelled out the door, interrupting the tense moment.

"Gladly" Viv said stiffly, brushing past Gina to get to the ladder and out of the treehouse.

"Viv!" Gina said to the back of her red-haired friend.

Gina and Lottie watched as Viv made her way down the ladder.

"Lottie, what is wrong with her?" Gina pleaded.

"She just, we don't, I don't know" Lottie stammered looking flustered. "You've never defended Viola."

"I wasn't defending her; I was just saying she's been different. Why is that so horrible?" Gina said slapping her thighs in frustration.

"Because that sounds like you're being nice to her."

"What's wrong with that?"

"She's never been nice to us."

Gina didn't know what to make of this conversation, but felt depressed. What should have been a good time in their favorite place instead turned out the opposite.

Lottie also looked saddened, and turned to the ladder to climb down after Viv.

With no one left, Gina grabbed the ladder railing to start down herself, mad at everything.

"Did something happen out there?" Alana asked after Lottie and Viv left the house.

Gina looked at Alana without saying anything. She was alternating between wanting to scream and wanting to cry.

"Why do you ask?"

"Viv hardly said a word except goodbye to me when she decided to wait outside on the driveway for her mom, and Lottie was silent and barely looked at you when she left" Alana continued.

"First, they, actually Viv, started acting like Viola and I are best friends just because I said that Viola has been different in rehearsals and might have helped me with my turns. Then Viv turned it into something more because she made it seem like we're friends because we're doing Dew Drop, and that she isn't because she isn't good enough. Oh…and in the middle of this, Viola was somehow here under the treehouse listening or spying on us or something."

"Viola was here?"

"Yes, we saw that pink coat going into the hedge at the back of the yard."

"Why would Viola be here?"

"I don't know!" Gina said in a louder voice, her upturned palms waving frantically up and down. "She heard us talking about going up into the treehouse earlier. Maybe she wanted to talk about Dew Drop and came over but decided to go home instead in the last minute."

"Why would she want to talk about Dew Drop?"

"Mom, I can't explain it. And that's what I was trying to get across to Viv and Lottie. She seems like a different person when we're alone in the room together, and it seemed like she wanted to tell me something earlier, but Miss Monopoly interrupted us. She's also never really spoken to me, let alone sided with me or helped me."

Gina plopped down into a kitchen chair and tried to wrap her brain around a strange thought: *Could I actually maybe like Viola a little bit? And if I do, what would that do to my friendship with Lottie and Viv?*

Chapter Sixteen

Gina felt nervous the following Monday. This was the National Ballet performance week which normally should have been exciting. Instead, Gina saw it as one notch closer to their own performance and the scholarship decision. On top of that, she had not heard from Lottie or Viv the rest of the weekend after the tree-house get together, and felt uneasy about seeing them. Seeing them standing at school that morning, Gina wanted to slip away unnoticed into her homeroom class.
This is crazy; they're my best friends.
Gina walked up and said "Hi" in a cheery voice, which was in contrast to her inner fear.
"Hi Gina" Lottie said looking unsure back and forth between Gina and Viv.
"Hi Viv" Gina said directly to Viv.
"Hi Gina, I wasn't sure if you would be talking to me today" Viv said in a soft voice. "I'm sorry about the things I said last weekend. I just, it's just, I don't know how to explain it" she said flustered. "We've been friends forever, and we've always disliked Viola, and now suddenly you're not disliking her so much anymore" she continued folding her arms across her chest. "And what's worse, you get to do a really good part, which you share with her, which I'll never get the chance to be considered for…and I'm jealous. Jealous of all of it."
"Viv" Gina interrupted, "first of all, I'm not sharing a part with Viola, I'm her understudy. I probably won't get to do that part either, if that's any consolation."
"Yes, but you should be. You dance with more passion that Viola, and have the elegance and beauty that I just don't have."
Taking a step closer to Viv, Gina said tilting her head "you've seen me fall, correct?"

Gina watched as Viv smiled. The tension broke a little.

"Viv, you and Lottie are my best friends. As I said in the treehouse, Viola HAS been different. And I'd be lying if I said I didn't respect her somehow in those rehearsal periods. She has been prepared; she has danced it beautifully even if she is cold with no emotion. She even helped me figure out why my turns weren't working, but I don't get the feeling she wants to be friends in any way. She still barely looks at me."

Gina didn't know what else to offer. Viv took a moment to think about this, and then asked "Why do you think she was at your house on Saturday?"

"I don't know; it's the last thing I would have expected. I certainly didn't invite her if that's what you're thinking."

"No, I didn't think that. I'm sorry again Gina."

Without saying anything, Gina moved in to give Viv a hug.

"I'm glad that's over" Lottie said relieved, a big smile spreading over her cheeks.

"What did you guys do the rest of the weekend?" Gina asked as she pulled away from Viv.

"We went holiday shopping" Lottie said.

"So did we" added Viv. "How about you Gina?"

"We decorated our house" Gina replied happily. Gina loved the way holiday decorations looked when unveiled again each year. The Peabodys put blue lights on the bushes outside their house, and Thomas always climbed on the roof to hang clear icicle lights that hung down over the house. Inside, the Peabody Christmas tree sparkled with white lights, and Alana had an assortment of (of all things!) Nutcracker dolls that she displayed in different nooks and crannies.

"Did your mom put the elf out?" Viv asked.

"Not yet, but soon" Gina replied. The Peabody elf was a holiday tradition that had captured Gina's sense of magic. Alana and Thomas had purchased an elf doll which they would put in ridiculous places with notes to Gina late each night after Gina had gone to bed. Gina would awaken every morning to look where the elf was next, and often found him in the refrigerator eating, or in the chimney stacking firewood, or even once trapped in her lunchbox with a note yelling for "HELP!" Gina loved believing in the magic the elf represented. Now that she was older, she helped Alana and Thomas think of places to put the elf in for Benny's enjoyment.

"Wow, the performance is this week already!" Lottie said changing the subject.

"We also start the put togethers in rehearsals this week" added Viv.

"Oh' that's right" Gina remembered. Gina didn't know how she felt about this, as the put togethers were full run throughs of the ballet where everyone finally was in the same room and had the chance to see each other dance. Gina felt ready for snow, and even though the Daffodil part was small, she felt slightly nervous for everyone to see her dance. Though, she had to admit, it was a fun kind of nervous, rather than a scary type of nervous.

Please don't let me have one of my monumental falls.

Before any more could be said, the homeroom warning bell sounded.

"See you guys later" Gina said backing away. Before she could turn completely around, she felt herself bump solidly into the person standing right behind her.

"Hi Gina."

Gina knew the voice before she completed the microscopic turn of her body.

"Hi Jake."

Out of the corner of her eye, she caught Lottie and Viv watching.

"How was your weekend?"

Gina gulped, and then said evenly "it was good. How was yours?"

"Busy. I had basketball practice all day Saturday, and then we had company come over for most of yesterday."

Thinking fast, Gina surprised herself by asking "when does the season start up?"

"Soon" Jake replied. "Our games start right after we come back from Christmas break."

"I better get to homeroom." Gina finished the conversation.

"Hope to see you at the performance Friday night" Jake said watching Gina start down the hall."

"I hope so too" Gina said turning around.

Walking the rest of the corridor, Gina smiled realizing that she actually said something valid, even though she really didn't have much interest in basketball, or its season for that matter.

She also smiled because she just liked Jake.

Chapter Seventeen

Gina was in a good mood when she arrived at ballet later that afternoon. Things seemed straightened out with her friends, she had talked to Jake earlier, and now there was a run through which seemed exciting at the moment.

"Maybe if I can find a private moment, I'll even ask Viola why she was in our backyard on Saturday" she thought as she walked into the dressing room to change into her dance clothes.

"Gina...don't freak out!"

"About what?" Gina said startled, turning to see Lottie running over to her.

"Mr. Stone is here!"

"Mr. Stone? As in Mr. Stone the Director of The National Ballet?"

"Yes!"

"Why is he here today? He's supposed to be here next week!"

"I overheard him telling Miss Angelica that there was some last-minute contract negotiation or something with the Grand Palace, and he had to fly in to deal with it today."

"Is he watching rehearsal?"

"Yes!"

"Wow...okay, well I think I'm ready."

"That's not all."

Gina looked blankly at Lottie, suddenly apprehensive.

"What else?"

"Viola's sick today, she's not here."

For a moment Gina stood still, not understanding why this new piece of information was important. Then it hit her.

Viola's sick.

Viola's not here today.

Viola won't be here to do Dew Drop.

Mr. Stone IS here though, and will have to watch the understudy in the run through.

Gina felt her insides squash with instant fear.

"Viv is already going over your Daffodil part" Lottie said softly, confirming Gina's dread.

Silence filled the room as Gina stared at Lottie.

"Gina, are you okay?"

"Yes, I'm fine" Gina said robotically as she began to automatically get dressed for class.

"Gina, you'll be fine; you're beautiful in everything you do" Lottie offered, placing a hand on Gina's shoulder in support.

"Lottie, this, THIS is a chance to impress Mr. Stone" Gina said turning to face Lottie. Worry lines had pulled her eyebrows up together like a puppet. "Normally, I would be preparing for a long time before this kind of opportunity. I feel totally off guard. I wish I would have known so I could have practiced more, or mentally gone through all my corrections more, anything so it's not this kind of surprise with so much at stake."

Gina sat down pulling her toe shoes out of her bag. Her therabands, snagged and tangled with the shoes, also rushed out like mad snakes landing at her feet.

Lottie reached down to pick them up, and held them wriggling in front of Gina.

"Gina, you've been working and practicing for weeks now with these. You've gotten so much stronger, so I don't know how much more you could have practiced if you had in fact known Mr. Stone was going to be here today."

Gina looked at Lottie's concerned face, and tried to quiet her racing fear.

"You have passion, and now you're even stronger" Lottie continued shaking the elastic bands in front of Gina. Seeing it was having no impact, she finished with "even if you fall flat on your face, I'll still love you."

Looking at Lottie's softly smiling face, Gina's nerves calmed a little bit.

"Thanks Lottie…oh my god!"

Gina finished getting ready, took a deep breath, and headed to the studio with Lottie.

Halfway down the hallway, they were interrupted by Viv rushing down the opposite way.

"Did Lottie tell you?"

"Yes!" Gina replied. "Are you good with Daffodil?"

"Yeah. I won't be as good as you, but I know it. Are you ready for Dew?"

"I don't know; I hope so!"

The three entered the studio, where another surprise awaited them; Mr. Stone was already seated in the room, apparently there to watch class as well. The studio, usually filled with different conversations before the start of class, was silent, as if someone had pressed mute. Gina looked over at Lottie and Viv in soundless understanding, and tip toed her way to her usual place at the barre.

"Hello dancers!" Miss Angelica's voice rang out as she suddenly entered the room, shattering the otherworldly scene. "As you can see, we have a very special guest: Mr. Stone, the Director of The National Ballet. Please join me in welcoming him!"

At this cue, Miss Angelica beamed her sunniest smile in his direction, and began to clap. Everyone responded by clapping as well, both in enthusiasm, and in relief to break the silence.

Mr. Stone stood up, waving his hand to signal that the applause was not necessary.

"I'm very happy to be here" he said in a surprisingly normal friendly voice. "Angelica, I must say, this is one of the quietest groups I've encountered in a while" he stated, turning to face his friend.

"They're a focused group" she said with a triumphant nod of her head at her students.

"I can see that" he replied back as he started to lower himself back into the chair.

Before he made it back into the chair, Mr. Stone suddenly popped back up like an adult jack-in-the-box.

"Actually, why don't I teach the class?"

Miss Angelica's eyes widened.

"REALLY?" she said a bit louder than she probably wanted to.

"Yes, I would love to, how about it?"

"We would be so honored, yes, …YES!"

With that, Mr. Stone walked over to one of the barres in the center, and addressed the dancers.

"I promise I'll go easy. Well, sort of easy" he said with a wink. And on that note, he began the plie combination, the first traditional ballet exercise.

Gina reached over and put her hand on the barre, focused on the exact steps Mr. Stone was demonstrating for them to do. As the music began, she began doing the movements almost on automatic; her brain just needed to figure out the specific patterns, her body flowed into the familiar movements seamlessly. Halfway through the barre exercises, it dawned on her that this was an extraordinary experience.

I'm taking class from the Director of The National Ballet. He is literally standing so close that I could reach out and touch his arm as he walks by me making the rounds looking at all of us. I wonder if this is one of the same classes that the dancers in the company get?

This realization filled Gina with a rush of adrenaline that started at her feet and spread up through her body like a shaft of sunlight chasing shadows away. She was so captivated that she synced completely with the music, almost as though she became a visible melody tracing designs in space.

Out of the corner of her eye, Gina thought she glimpsed Mr. Stone watching her. She immediately focused straight ahead, not wanting to know for sure; she preferred to imagine that he WAS watching her.

Was he looking at me?

As if on cue, Lottie whispered to Gina "he's watching you!" when they finished the barre and were allowed one minute for a water break.

He was looking at me!

Gina felt buoyant as she had felt strong throughout the barre.

I hope I don't mess up now in the center combinations.

The class reorganized in the center of the room to begin the second part of class, which would include Gina's favorite section of class: the grande allegro big jumps. Unfortunately, her snarky nemesis, the pirouette or turn combinations, always preceded the jumping.

Mr. Stone began showing the first combination in the center, which was to be an adagio phrase. Gina had always liked this part of class, as it was a slow set of steps that showcased high extensions of the legs, and allowed artistry and feeling to really be used. This was another trait that Gina excelled at, and why everyone always remarked that she danced with so much passion. This was also what Viola lacked, and Gina was suddenly disappointed that Viola was not there so that she could show off this skill standing next to Viola who usually danced so barren. This might have improved her chances at being considered for one of the eventual scholarships. Before she could dwell on this, she also vividly remembered that Viola not being here also meant she was doing Dew Drop a little while later, which kicked her back to reality.

Gina walked forward when Mr. Stone asked for the first group to show the exercise, and took a spot in front. As the music began, she again thought that he was looking over in her direction, but didn't want to be obvious by looking back his way to check. Once again, Gina surrendered herself to the music, and stretched her long limbs to their extreme alongside the harmony playing.

She felt good about the adagio when she finished and walked away.

The next combination was an intricate tendue, or stretching of the feet in different patterns and directions. This was a piece of cake, as far as Gina was concerned, as it posed no threats of falling off balance or other demons.

As she waited for group two to finish the tendue combination, Gina realized that pirouettes would be next.

Ugh, here they come. Please let me stay vertical.

Mr. Stone walked to the corner of the room, and began to trace a long waltzing pirouette combination that literally moved all over the room. It had quite a few turns in it, Gina realized, and deduced that she would have to be extra careful in her preparations as they would come while traveling across the studio.

Gina got into position for the first group, thoughts of foot placement and staying on balance bombarding her brain. As she moved with the group, she felt

small.

This thought, along with the not falling thoughts (which seemed to be attached to some sort of boomerang) continued to assault her thoughts, and she felt even

smaller.

She hesitated before the first turn sequence, but did not fall

"Not perfect, but I'm still upright" she thought a little shakily.

The second set of turns also were not quite on balance, but she still did not fall.

Gina finished the last part of the phrase along with the last set of turns, and was relieved to be done.

Before the second group could begin, the music suddenly stopped.

Gina looked over, and saw that Mr. Stone had pressed stop on the disc, and was whispering something to Miss Angelica who had leaned ever so close to his ear.

To Gina's horror, they both looked over briefly in her direction, and then resumed their hushed discussion.

After what seemed like a year in time, Mr. Stone leaned away from Miss Angelica's silent movie mouth and looked straight at Gina and said

"Miss Peabody…"

Time stood still for Gina, who felt abandoned on some cliff of impending anxiety waiting for Mr. Stone to continue.

Looking quickly back at Miss Angelica nodding softly to reaffirm that her name was indeed Peabody, Mr. Stone continued.

"Miss Peabody, I'm confused" he said walking over towards her. "I've admired your grace and passion since we began class, but it was as if there was another Gina Peabody doing this particular turn combination. Where did all that delicious passion go?"

Gina stared back at Mr. Stone's upturned questioning palms, and didn't know how to respond.

"Who cares if there are scary things in any combination?" he continued. "What is most important, is that you enjoy dancing no matter what. Because then, and only then, will your audience also get to experience the joy of moving through you. If you break down and take the passion away, they will also feel that loss and then our jobs as dancers will be incomplete. If you fall, you fall. We all do at some point. Audiences will forgive a fall, but still admire you if you continue with the same beautiful excitement. If you snatch that away, they will feel empty and disappointed."

Gina nodded her head to all he was saying, and felt guilty that she had let her thoughts of falling ruin her streak of self-assurance. Worse, she also felt as though she was somehow standing in some kind of invisible spotlight with all eyes on her.

"Why don't you repeat this again with group two" he suggested. His waving hand gestured Gina back to the original diagonal to take a spot with group two.

Gina walked over and stood next to Lottie, who winked at her in solidarity. As the music began, she drove all intellectual thoughts out of her mind, and let herself just *feel*. Since the phrase moved all across the floor, Gina glided larger,

Larger

LARGER.

She sailed through the air feeling like a silk scarf wafting with a warm breeze which pulled it here and there.

When she finished, she looked over and saw Miss Angelica smiling. Mr. Stone looked triumphant and said "There we go. That's what the dance world will expect."

Gina smiled back, ridiculously happy that Mr. Stone had noticed her, given her feedback, and that she had somehow succeeded in applying his correction to her dancing. She also knew that all that was left was the big jumps, which she not only didn't fear, but relished.

Mr. Stone gave a big series of jumps, which Gina eagerly attacked with zest and lightning precision. Though he didn't necessarily solely watch her, Gina felt that he continued to monitor how she was doing. When class finished, he addressed the class as a whole.

"Well done students! I see my friend Miss Angelica has trained you professionally and beautifully. I'm looking forward to seeing your run through today, as well as seeing you all on stage after our show this week."

The class, including Gina, applauded, and then Miss Angelica said "let's take a small break, and start the run-through in 20 minutes." With that, she and Mr. Stone walked away once again in whispering tones, a private conversation that Gina would have paid to hear.

"He was amazing" Viv said as they made their way to their bags to get their pointe shoes on.

"And so nice!" Lottie added pulling out her shoes.

Gina guzzled some water, and could only get out "I know" between huge gulps.

All three quickly got their pointe shoes on, and without having to be told, scampered to the barre to warm up their feet. In the middle of this quick preparation, Miss Monopoly's clicking high heels made their way over to Gina.

"Gina, you are aware that Viola is not here today and that you doing Dew, correct?"

"Yes, I know."

"Good. I'm sure you will not embarrass us."

Gina's mood fell as Miss Monopoly clicked her way away.

"Why would she say THAT?" Gina asked turning to her friends.

"She's just making sure you'll be ready" Viv said encouragingly.

"Well, that didn't help" Gina said despondently.

"Don't worry, Mr. Stone already noticed you, and obviously is interested in your dancing" Lottie added.

Sensing Gina suddenly felt insecure, Lottie continued "Gina, remember what he said: don't lose your passion because of nerves. He said it didn't matter if anyone fell, so that's not so important to him."

Putting her hand out to finish, Lottie added "don't let Monopoly ruin it for you."

It was hard for Gina to feel assured in this moment. Her brain told her Lottie was right. Her fear told her other things, and coaxed an army of fresh nerves to assemble.

Chapter Eighteen

"Okay, I heard from the other moms. Now that we're in the car, tell me all about it!"

Gina saw Alana's impatience as she finished waving goodbye to everyone and got into their car. Slamming the door shut, she leaned forward and exclaimed "Oh my god, it was crazy!"

"Tell me!"

Gina recanted most of the day leading up to the run-through while Alana drove.

"And what happened when you ran the ballet for him?"

"Well, thankfully Snow was first, because I was nervous for Dew Drop and as always, getting out there and dancing with everyone to begin with helped me to relax a little. Then, when Flowers started, I remembered what Mr. Stone had said, and thought if I fall, I fall, but I want him to notice me, and Viola not being here is my big chance."

Gina stopped for a moment to think how to exactly say her next sentence.

"Mom...I think I was really good."

Gina retold her Dew Drop experience almost as if it was someone else's story. Her face became illuminated with enthusiasm while she told Alana what had happened.

"We started Flowers, and first, Viv and Lottie danced amazingly, especially Lottie. I've never seen her dance with such spitfire precision in her Carnation solo; it was as if we all got some superhuman strength by having Mr. Stone watching. Lottie's always been good at turning, but she whipped off more turns than ever today. Viv did really good in Daffodil too, but that part doesn't do very much, so she didn't get the opportunity to really show off. Then, my music came, and Mom, something really strong took over my body. I felt as though my arms, my legs, all of my body was so connected; it felt like I could control everything and anything. When I entered and knew Mr. Stone was watching, I suddenly wanted to show off. It was a chance I didn't expect, and was so scary and fun at the same time.

Gina fished around in her bag to find her water bottle and took a sip.

"When it got time for the turns, my foot remembered how to place itself down on the floor to push off, and all my turns from that point on were pretty solid. Not as great as Lottie's, but solid for me."

"Maybe those theraband exercises helped" Alana interrupted.

"For sure, I think so. Anyway, when I finished, everyone clapped, and Mr. Stone smiled and nodded at me. I heard him tell Miss Angelica that "if the understudy is that good in the part, I can't wait to see the first cast dancer."

Gina looked over Alana's shoulder and said in an eager voice "Maybe I made a good enough impression for one of the New York spots."

"Gina, I know how much you would want that. But remember, your Dad hasn't said yes yet."

"Mom, he HAS to let me go if I get offered one of the spots. Today's class and rehearsal made me want it even more."

Gina's mood was so uplifted that she pushed away the possibility of Thomas saying no. Her dreams were too big to be squashed right now.

Before she knew it, it was Thursday, one day before The National Ballet's performance. After Monday's rehearsal with Mr. Stone, the rest of the week had been routine, except everyone complimented Gina and Lottie on their dancing, a lot. Everyone also somehow let Viola know that Gina had done exceptionally well the day she was absent. Gina expected Viola to say something, but she was silent and neutral as always. Most of the school was eagerly waiting for the National Ballet performance on Friday night, if anything, it meant they all had the night off of dancing themselves. Miss Angelica took time Thursday night to remind all the students that they should dress nicely for the performance (check! thought Gina), and that she looked forward to seeing them the next night at The Grand Palace Theater.

"I'm glad we're not dancing tomorrow" Gina said as she got home after rehearsal. "My body feels tired."

"Go take a bubble bath, and I'll get dinner on the table" Alana said to Gina.

"What's for dinner tonight" Gina asked as she made her way out of the kitchen.

"Homemade chicken soup, salad and warm cornbread" Alana answered.

"Perfect" uttered Gina as she walked towards her bathroom, followed by Stella.

Gina walked into the bathroom, and opened the cupboard to choose either the yellow or pink bubble bath to pour into the tub. She didn't expect to see a new bottle standing next to the yellow and pink one; it was orange, and when Gina lifted it out, she saw its name was "Daffodil!"

"Mom, did you buy me new bubble bath?" Gina yelled out from upstairs.

"Yes, I couldn't resist when I saw that name today!" Alana shouted up.

"Thanks!" Gina hollered back as she closed the door again. All the raised voices caused Stella to wag her tail furiously, and to run around the bathroom.

"Okay, okay, down girl" Gina whispered to Stella, calming the dog so she could start running the water for the bath. Opening the bottle, Gina poured an extra amount of the orange liquid out of the container. Soon piles and piles of bubbles rose out of the water like puffy mountains. It smelled like tangerines.

Gina slipped into the hot bubbled water letting her hands skim the top, pushing the piles here and there.

She imagined all the beautiful things ahead for tomorrow, and when her mind settled on dinner at Papa Lou's, her stomach howled in response.

Gina got out on that cue, toweled off and made her way down to the kitchen.

"I smell oranges" Benny said as she sat down in her chair.

Chapter Nineteen

Gina woke up Friday morning earlier than when her alarm was set for. She rolled over to look at the clock, and then rolled back over to lay for a few minutes, thinking about the day and night ahead.

School's done at 3:00, we'll be home by 3:15, so that gives me two hours at least to get ready before we have to leave for dinner.

Happy with that timetable, Gina got out of bed and went into the kitchen.

"You're up early" Alana said pouring a cup of coffee.

"I know, go figure."

"Good morning Gina" Thomas said walking in freshly shaved.

"Hi Dad."

Gina watched her father get a cup of coffee as well, and head over to the table opening the newspaper. He patted Stella on the head with a smile, leading Gina to think he was in a good mood this morning.

"Dad, remember when mom told you about Monday's rehearsal?"

Looking quizzical, Thomas looked up from the paper.

"Yes, I do; it seems like you made a good impression on this Mr. Stone."

Sitting down next to him, Gina took a deep breath, and said "I've gone through that rehearsal every day since Monday. I keep thinking about it because it made me feel special. Mr. Stone made me feel special. Having all my friends see me dance the way I danced made me feel special. Seeing Miss Angelica smiling made me feel special."

Gina noted that Thomas was maybe actually listening to her, rather than continuing to read the paper while she was talking. Seizing this moment, she paused (for dramatic effect, she hoped) and continued.

"It made me really happy."

"I'm glad it made you happy Gina."

"It would make me really happy to take a spot in New York if I'm offered one."

"We've had this discussion Gina, and you know my feelings on this subject" he replied, his gaze reverting back into the pages.

"Dad, I do, but do you really know mine?"

Silence filled the kitchen. Gina stared at Thomas, who either pretended or actually continued to read the paper back in front of his eyes.

"Gina, it's time for you to get ready for school" Alana said quietly.

Gina looked over to Alana, who was pointing her head in the direction of Gina's room. Gina got up and followed her gaze out. As she left, she looked back and saw Alana sitting down and softly pulling the newspaper out of Thomas's grasp.

Arriving at school, Gina quickly looked for Lottie and Viv before classes started, and found them waiting for her in the common area just outside the cafeteria.

"Hi Gina!" Lottie cried out. "Ready for tonight?"

"Yes" Gina said unenthusiastically.

"What's wrong?" Lottie said immediately.

"My dad still won't talk about New York. He just doesn't get it. It won't matter if I get a spot because even if I do, I don't think he'll let me go. I tried to bring it up again this morning, but he tuned me out the minute I mentioned the scholarships."

Gina paced in place; it was so frustrating.

Gina saw that Lottie and Viv didn't know what to say. She knew that Lottie's parents would let her go if she were to get a spot, and Viv wasn't expecting to be offered one. They looked sorry for her, making her feel awkward.

The warning bell for homeroom rang, saving all of them from their loss for words.

"See you at lunch" Gina said, turning away to go to her classroom.

Gina thought about options she might be able to give to Thomas in a last-ditch effort to convince him.

Maybe if Lottie goes, the Tuddeldums could talk to him, reassuring him that we would be there together.

Possible, but not strong.

Maybe Mom could somehow go too.

Unlikely, Benny needs her here.

Maybe if Miss Angelica goes, I could stay with her.

Even more unlikely, she has her own summer session.

As lunch approached, Gina hadn't come up with a good plan to consider. They all seemed farfetched.

Finding Lottie and Viv in the cafeteria, the three of them took out their lunches from their backpacks.

"Gina," Lottie said as she tackled a huge meatloaf sandwich stuck in a hamburger bun, "if you get a spot, we can ask Miss Angelica to ask Mr. Stone to talk to your Dad."

"Maybe, but I think if anyone will be able to convince him, it will be my mom."

"Lottie, that's the biggest sandwich!" Viv said across the table. Looking up, Gina stared wide eyed at the big piece of loaf coming out each side of the bun.

"I know" Lottie giggled, "I guess my mom wanted to get rid of leftovers."

Gina and Viv started laughing as they watched Lottie open her mouth wider than they'd ever seen.

'You look like a shark" Gina said.

"Or a whale" Viv cried.

Lottie started laughing at this, helping Gina's mood uplift some.

When they'd settled down, Gina said "My parents said we're meeting at Papa Lou's at 5:30."

"I know, my folks said the same" replied Viv.

Lottie only nodded, as her mouth was so full of meatloaf. This made Gina and Viv start laughing all over again.

Viv looked towards Lottie and said one last time "you *ARE* a whale!" Finishing up, they got up to leave.

"See you guys tonight" Gina said.

Gina watched Lottie swallow hard, and held up her hand waving goodbye for the moment. As she walked to her next class, she realized that she had the performance tonight to look forward to. Lost in these thoughts, she rounded a corner and saw Jake walking towards her.

"Hi Gina!"

"Hi."

"Amanda can't stop talking about you; she said you were so good in some rehearsal. You're her idol now."

"Really?"

"Really!"

Jake smiled at her, and Gina replied "That's so sweet, I've never been someone's idol!"

"See you at the performance tonight" he finished, smiling one more time before heading his own way.

Gina suddenly felt better.

"I WAS good!"

Her mood improved, and now she was eager to get through the rest of school.

Gina began to get impatient towards the rest of the day. Her face broke into relief when the last bell of the day finally rang. She grabbed her backpack, and ran out into the hall with all the other students like a giant race.

Leaping out the doors, Gina looked right and left for Alana. Running to the car, Gina literally threw the back door open to jump inside.

"Hi Mom!" Gina blurted out as she furiously got her seat belt clicked.

"Hi Gina, how was school?"

"It was fine; too long, but Jake told me I'm Amanda's new idol!"

" What, he did?"

"He did! I ran into him, and he said since my Dew rehearsal, she's my new fan. Did you have any luck with Dad this morning when I left?"

"Not a lot, but he's not horribly saying absolutely no like he did a few weeks ago. Or maybe he's just quiet, I don't know" Alana said.

Gina didn't risk her luck asking more. Not saying absolutely no was a start, a wedge that she could maybe work with, given the right tools. Perhaps the grandeur of tonight's performance might dent his perspective.

Pulling into the driveway, Alana barely had time to put the car into "park" when she heard the "Click" of the seatbelt being released. Gina ran to the garage door before Alana had even pulled her keys out of the ignition.

Gina quickly pressed in the code numbers of the garage door, and watched the slow lifting of the door to let her inside. Ducking under the half- opened door, she ran through to the inside door and disappeared with a "Hello Stella" as she made her way into the house.

Chapter Twenty

Gina ran into the kitchen to grab something small to eat, and sat down with a yogurt parfait swiped from the refrigerator. Feeling generous because of her good mood, she made an effort to be nice to Benny, who came in to sit next to her and asked for some of her snack. Though it usually annoyed her to share, she silently got up to get an extra spoon so he could have some. As he dug huge pits into her smooth confection, she began to regret her kindness.

"Gina, did you see my new video game?" Benny asked between rapid swallows.

"No."

"Here, look."

Benny pulled his game across the counter, and Gina reluctantly found herself absorbed into a magical land of knights and sorcerers.

"Gina, you do realize that we have to leave in about an hour, don't you?" Gina suddenly heard Alana state from across the room.

Looking up at the clock, Gina was irritated that Benny's game had altered her exact timeline planning. She nodded affirmative to Alana, and ran to her room to get ready.

Hair up or hair down?

Gina went to her mirror and began to play with putting her hair into different styles. First was the classic bun she wore every day to ballet.

Too much like class.

Next, she tried it just down.

Too messy looking.

She pulled her hair back into a ponytail trying to decide what to try next, but stopped to take a second look.

"The ponytail actually looks pretty good" she unexpectedly realized, and said out loud to Stella who had wandered in.

Finishing her hair, Gina went into her closet and pulled out the dark green velvet dress, slipped it on, and tied the black sash around her waist. Facing the mirror, she turned this way and that looking at the dress at all angles. Gina loved this dress; the dark green of the velvet not only felt wonderful to the touch, but it made her eyes look emerald green. Happy with the choice, she looted her messy jewelry box for a pair of earrings to match. While she dug through the tangled mess searching, she heard Alana holler "Gina, it's almost time to leave soon, are you almost ready?"

"Yes Mom!"

Gina picked up a small black purse and dropped a small brush, lip balm, and a few mints in.

Ready.

Walking into the family room, Gina saw Alana and Thomas talking to Mrs. Bumble, who had come to watch Benny for the night.

Gina entered just in time to hear Miss Bea say "Well Mr. Benjamin, I sincerely hope you will help me make my famous peanut butter cookies."

At this mere mention of sweets, Benny dropped his action figure toy and began to jump up and down.

"YES MA'AM!"

Gina giggled at his enthusiasm, causing everyone to turn in her direction.

Everyone got quiet as they looked at Gina standing in the doorway.

"What's wrong?" Gina asked.

"Gina, you're beautiful" Alana said warmly, with unexpected tears filling her eyes.

"And so grown up" Thomas added. "Are you sure you're the accident prone one?" he jokingly asked.

Gina saw Thomas was looking at her differently, and hoped it was somehow a good sign.

"Thanks" Gina replied back to them.

Gina went to the hall closet to get her jacket, and heard Alana say a few last words to Mrs. Bumble and then to Benny "You behave for Miss Bea young man, ok?"

"Bye Benny" Gina said on her way to the garage. Benny was already so absorbed playing his game again that he did not even hear his sister say goodbye.

Gina got in the car, followed by her parents. She felt hungry again, and thought about those pizzas.

Please don't let me drop any pizza on this dress.

Chapter Twenty-One

The Peabodys arrived at Papa Lou's and quickly saw the Tuddeldums and Snapples in the back of the crowded room.

"Wow, a lot of people tonight; I wonder if they are all going to the show?" Gina thought as she made her way through the jungle of seated customers. Heading towards Lottie and Viv, Gina stumbled to avoid tripping over a woman who suddenly pulled her chair out from a table. To her horror, she almost took a nose dive not one minute into the restaurant. Catching herself from falling head first, she regained her balance, but the sash on her dress got caught around the back of the woman's chair. As she righted herself, she heard a rip in the fabric, and saw the snap holding the sash to the dress on her left side vault out into the air like a tennis ball in one of those automatic feeder machines. Gina regained her balance, and looked down to inspect the damage.

Oh my god, my dress!

Standing in the middle of the noisy room, ridiculously obvious to all, but entirely not noticed because of all the commotion, Gina looked at the sagging sash now hanging from her dress. Turning to find Alana not two steps behind her, Gina gestured to her injured clothing, and saw Alana's eyes widen in surprise. In an improvisational silent dance, Gina was partnered by Alana's driving hands towards their table to assess the tear.

"Oh Mom, my favorite dress!"

"Gina, how did this happen; we just got here!"

"I tripped over that woman's chair, and my dress got caught!"

Looking over, Gina saw that Lottie and Viv were watching this pantomime and understood the drama. Seeing the hanging sash, Gina felt embarrassed.

With nothing left to do, Gina felt Alana rip the sash from remaining snap on her right side, releasing it entirely. She reached across and tied it manually around Gina's waist, where it hung again, but not form fitting, or as glamorous as it formerly was. In fact, it looked frumpy.

"We'll fix it tomorrow" Alana said to Gina.

Sitting down, Gina asked Lottie "Does it look bad?"

"No, you really wouldn't know; it's just looser than when it was attached" Lottie replied, staring at the big bow it created.

"Viv?" Gina asked, knowing Viv would tell the honest truth.

"Its fine, you still look great, good catch by the way. I thought you were going straight to the floor" Viv answered.

"You saw?"

"Umm, yeah. You're lucky you're still wearing a dress" Viv said jokingly.

"That stupid chair!" Gina blurted out just as a menu was thrust in front of her face. Papa Lou, of Papa Lou's had waddled over.

"Ahh some of my favorite customers…and what pretty young ladies we have here tonight!"

Gina looked over her shoulder at the smiling Papa Lou. His grin was almost entirely hidden by one of the largest mustaches Gina had ever seen. It was his trademark, and always made Gina think he looked like a giant walrus.

"Hi Papa Lou."

Papa Lou patted Gina's hair in response to her hello, causing her to lean forward lest he continue patting and mess her hair.

I don't need that ruined too.

"Girls, why don't you three split a pizza" Alana hollered over the din of the room.

Gina nodded, and turned her attention back to the menu.

"How about one with everything; the number one called the works?" she asked.

"No, I don't want pizza meat" Viv replied.

"How about the vegetarian one then?" Gina countered.

"Too much green" Lottie said back.

"Ladies, we can split it three ways" Papa Lou offered, overhearing them disagree on the pie.

"Great, I'll have the works on my third" Gina said.

"Vegetarian" Viv said.

"Just plain with cheese" Lottie finished.

"Plain?" Gina replied to Lottie.

"Yeah, I like the cheese."

"That's weird" Gina said, squeezing her eyebrows and pinching her nose in response.

"Why is that weird?" Lottie said a little defensive.

"Because there's so many options."

"Maybe I don't want the options, and what do you care what I have on my portion anyway?"

Gina realized Lottie was right as she actually didn't have a good rebuttal.

"Sorry Lottie, I'm mad about my dress."

Lottie let Gina dangle a second or two before finally saying "Okay."

"Gina, how's Jake?" Viv said changing the subject.

"What do you mean?"

"We saw you talking down the hall at school today."

Gina wished all aspects of her life were as interesting to her friends as Jake apparently was, but unfortunately, she had nothing to report.

"He only wanted to know if I'll be at the performance tonight."

"Oh."

"And now in a less than stellar fashion statement." Gina instinctively left out the part that he had said that she was Amanda's new idol. She knew it wouldn't come out right. And some part of her wanted to keep that intel just for herself; her private wonderful secret.

"Just stay seated all night" Viv joked. "That way no one will be able to see the sash."

"That's not going to happen" Gina said taking a sip of water. "Unless I sit through intermission."

"And until everyone leaves after the show" Lottie added with a slight laugh.

Gina thought about the absurdity of her just sitting there, and began to laugh as well. Her mood lifted.

"Where are you guys sitting?" Gina asked.

"I don't know, I didn't ask" Lottie responded.

"We're somewhere near the front of the stage I think" Viv added.

"I hope we're somewhere in the middle with no one nearby opening candy with that crackling sound" Gina said looking towards the doors leading to the kitchen.

I hope the pizza gets here soon, I'm really hungry.

"Or next to someone who hogs the armrest" Viv said.

"I wish we were sitting together" Gina said, spying Papa Lou emerging from the swinging doors carrying large plates towards their table.

"I know, I wish we were sitting together too" Lottie finished, gaping at the pizza that was placed on their table.

Gina looked down at the bubbling perfection sitting in front of her, and eagerly reached across to pull a slice of the works out from the perfect circle.

Yum.

Lottie and Viv each tugged at their portions as well, and all three were immediately consumed by the meal. Gina stopped talking to appreciate the taste of each item included in the work's: sausage, pepperoni, onion, green pepper and olive. Her eyes continually looking upward matched her "oohs" and "ahhs." It was a kaleidoscope of savory flavors.

Lottie and Viv closed their eyes with accompanying murmurs to join Gina in the delicious food choreographic study.

Each ate all the slices of their respective parts of the pie, and each sat back stuffed when done.

"I'm a whale" Lottie said from her reclined position.

"For sure, especially after your meatloaf sandwich earlier!" Viv said over the table.

Gina thought Lottie would find something funny to say back, but she only raised her hand up in a "thumbs up agreement" to Viv.

Gina smiled watching Lottie agree that she was a whale. She really wished that they were in fact sitting together so they could whisper and compare notes about the dancing.

Looking over at the adults, Gina saw that they also had sat back in their chairs with smiles on their faces. They were also done, and no one was moving except for Thomas waving for the check.

"I guess we're leaving soon" Gina said to her friends.

"Well, we should" Viv replied back, "it's already 6:45."

Gina looked up and saw it was in fact only 45 minutes till the performance. "That went by fast" she thought as she gathered up her loose sash.

Too bad I'm not more of a whale, at least the sash would be tighter around my waist.

The group gathered waiting for the bill to be paid, and then dodged their way out of the still crowded restaurant. Gina peeled her eyes wary for any more chairs to suddenly trip her up again.

Making their way safely outside with no more mishaps, Gina turned to her friends.

"See you soon!"

Chapter Twenty-Two

The Grand Palace Theater was every bit as beautiful as Gina remembered it to be. Walking into the majestic lobby, Gina was happy to see so many people. She felt like she was part of something big.

"There is so much energy in this room" she thought again. She looked over the crowds hoping to see Lottie or Viv, but there were just too many people for her to find her friends.

"I wonder if Lottie and Viv are here yet" Gina said to Alana.

"I don't know, but maybe we'll see them when we sit down."

"Hello Miss Peabody" Gina heard behind her, and recognized the crisp accent of Miss Monopoly.

"Hello Miss Monopoly" Gina answered back, turning around to see her teacher in one of the frilliest gowns she had ever seen. She instantly disliked the dress with what looked like a thousand white and green ruffles sticking out in every direction. She looked like a walking Christmas package. The feeling must have been mutual; she noted Miss Monopoly's eyes taking in the sagging sash around her waist.

"Are you excited for the performance?" she asked after her fashion assessment.

"Yes, of course" Gina replied back.

With all these people here, why do I have to run into her?

"I hope this will serve as a good inspiration to keep focused on your own dancing."

Duh.

Gina nodded, wanting Miss Monopoly to continue on through the lobby.

"I'm sure it will" was all she could get out.

"Enjoy" Miss Monopoly said with a smile, and then she and her collection of ruffles made their way through the crowd ready to catch more victims with "inspirational" notes.

Happy she was gone, Gina once again looked around the mob. She saw Jake in the distance, and her heart jolted slightly. Jake did not see her, so she was able to look at him uninterrupted. He looked very handsome dressed up. Normally, Gina saw Jake in either jeans or sweats, and had to admit, he looked pretty good in those clothes. But now, standing with his family in black jeans and a black sports jacket over a simple white t-shirt, he looked like one of those models you see walking through some museum in a fragrance commercial. He was talking to his sister Amanda, and Gina was endeared seeing how patiently he listened to his sister.

He's a keeper.

Before she could stalk watch him any longer, other people moved in front of her, barring any more views of him.

At least he didn't see me in this dress! Maybe I WILL stay seated.

Gina and her parents wove through the crowds towards the doors leading into the theater, and just when they had made it in, they ran into Miss Angelica standing elegantly in a simple black dress alongside Mr. Stone watching the many ticket holders pour into the space. Gina thought they made a handsome couple as they welcomed the public coming to the performance.

"Hello Gina" Miss Angelica said warmly as Gina stepped through the door. "Hello Alana, Thomas" she continued, "I'm happy to see you here. Eric, this is Alana and Thomas Peabody, Gina's parents" she said introducing them to the famous director.

"It's a pleasure to meet you" Mr. Stone generously replied, extending his hand out to shake Thomas's in greeting.

"The pleasure is ours: we've heard so much from Gina about your attendance at her rehearsal last Monday" Alana offered, as she also shook Mr. Stone's still extended hand.

'Ahh, yes, and hello Miss Peabody, it is even a greater pleasure to see you again" he finished, offering his hand respectfully, and maturely, down in Gina's direction.

Gina shook his hand, happy to make a further connection. Then to her delight, Mr. Stone turned to Thomas and said "You must be so very proud of your daughter. She impressed me with her talent and passion for dance. I think she's got real potential for something special in ballet."

Thomas was taken aback by this unexpected compliment, but then recovered by saying "thank you, we're always proud of Gina. She puts a lot of energy into everything, including dance."

"Well, it has certainly paid off" Eric added.

Gina waited for Thomas to continue with something, but he said nothing more, only smiling once again at Mr. Stone and Miss Angelica.

Alana broke in saying "we should probably go find out seats."

"Come backstage afterwards if you like" Mr. Stone said waving goodbye as he and Miss Angelica strolled towards more people coming in.

"Mom...can we?" Gina asked happily.

"We'll see when it's over" Alana answered back as Thomas led them out of the doorway.

They continued into the theater along with a lot of other eager people who were filing in and filling up rows like ants walking along the ground. They walked up to a friendly usher, who smiled and offered to show them to their seats.

The usher glanced at their numbers, and led them down one of the long aisles towards the middle of the theatre. Stopping, she gestured and said "Here we go, your seats are midway down this row, numbers 25, 26 and 27." Gina entered the narrow space first, and began walking looking down at the corresponding numbers, counting them up towards number 25. It was only when she got up to around 14 that she happened to take stock of her surroundings, and noticed Viola sitting in her row. She quickly calculated the remining number of seats, and realized too late that Viola must be in seat 28.

Of all the seats in this big theater, I'm sitting next to Viola.

Gina saw Viola look up at that second, seeing Gina headed towards her. She knew it was too late to reverse out, or to switch places with either Alana or Thomas as the space was too confined for any maneuvering, especially with Viola watching. It would have been too obvious.

To make matters more awkward, just as she got to her seat, she saw Viola's eyes do a Miss Monopoly sweep over her dress and its wayward sash.

"Hi Viola" Gina said a little too quickly, eager to sit and hide her dress.

"What happened to your dress?"

Too late.

"I tripped at Papa Lou's. My dress and a chair had an unexpected meeting." Gina said honestly.

Viola sat quietly for a second, and then laughed.

"It's not as bad as you probably think."

Gina sensed Viola was not making fun of her, leading her to then say while lifting the limp sash "I almost did a face plant in front of all those people. I'm lucky that this is all that happened."

Viola laughed again, and then turned away from Gina finishing with "Thanks Gina, now you've made my night interesting."

Gina looked over not knowing what Viola meant by that. Was she not interested to be there? She wanted to ask, but knew somehow that this wasn't the place or time. Looking beyond the now silent Viola, she saw her parents sitting on the other side of her. Gina once again marveled at how much her mom looked like Miss Angelica, and thought that what she had suspected for a while was probably true.

Viola's mom and Miss Angelica are sisters. Viola is Miss Angelica's niece.

Gina opened up her program, but was aware that Viola sat stoically while her parents seemed to be having a good time. She didn't want to look, but sensed that they were the ones wanting to be here, and that Viola was just, well, brought along against her will.

"This is so weird, especially if they're related" Gina thought as she pretended to be deep into the story of The Nutcracker, a ballet she knew inside out.

Gina's thoughts were suspended as the lights began flashing for the last straggling people to get in and to their seats. Gina looked around for Lottie and Viv, but didn't see them anywhere in the sea of heads. As the lights began to lower, there was a commotion at the front of the stage. The red velvet curtain parted, and Mr. Stone walked out to face everyone in the audience.

"Welcome to our production of The Nutcracker. My name is Eric Stone, and I am the Director of the company. We are so happy to bring this performance to you here at The Grand Palace Theater. I would like to bring out two of our leading dancers, Rosalie Bright and Logan Stark, who will dance the leading roles of the Sugar Plum Fairy and her Cavalier partner tonight."

Gina held her breath as a tall blonde woman and dark-haired man in practice ballet clothes walked out onto the stage. Even though the woman had on sweat pants, Gina could see that her hair was up in the traditional bun hairdo topped by a small sparkling crown. She also had on the pointe shoes like Gina and her friends wore in their classes with Miss Angelica.

"She looks beautiful" Gina murmured.

"Never mind about her, he's the beautiful one" Viola whispered in response.

Gina took a good look at Logan, and had to admit he was very good looking.

"Yes, he is" she quietly said in the hushed light.

Mr. Stone handed a microphone to the woman who smiled out to the audience and began to speak.

"Hello, my name is Rosalie Bright. Logan and I would like to thank you for supporting the arts, and coming to the ballet. We hope you enjoy the show."

Rosalie then handed the microphone over to Logan, who added before they left "Rosalie and I are happy that we will also be here to dance in Miss Wentworth's production next week. We hope to see you there." He flashed what had to be the whitest set of teeth to the audience, and then they went back behind the curtain.

"Our production just looked up" Viola said with a slight hint of enthusiasm.

Mr. Stone waited until the two dancers were gone, and then asked the audience "does anyone have any questions they would like to ask? After a brief pause where nobody raised their hands, he opened up his hands in a wide sweeping arc saying "this wonderful fairy tale ballet tells the story of a young girl named Clara who falls asleep at a holiday party and dreams about her toy Nutcracker and a magical Land of the Sweets. Happy holidays to all" the director concluded as he also then left the stage.

The lights then lowered completely, hushing any remaining noise in anticipation for the start of the show. In the darkness, the orchestra began playing the overture music. And just like that the big red curtain slowly rose.

Chapter Twenty-Three

Gina and the audience were instantly transported to the Stahlbaum house. The raised curtain revealed a giant living room filled with guests in beautiful dresses and suits dancing around a Christmas tree. Gina noticed a young girl in an especially pretty pink dress, who seemed to be in a spotlight.

That must be Clara, she doesn't look much older than me!

Clara looked beautiful in all her movements, especially when she had the special spotlight shining down on her. It was as though she was in a moonbeam.

I hope that can be me someday.

The remainder of this party scene unfolded with a lot of gesturing, the inevitable Nutcracker gift to Clara by her uncle Herr Drosselmeyer, and everyone eventually saying goodbye.

Gina enjoyed it, but found herself restless and ready for more action.

She didn't have to wait long. The ballet progressed into the next scene featuring the well-known battle scene between soldiers and mice under the large Christmas tree, with Clara asleep on a couch nearby.

Gina was amused as a giant mouse ran onstage, woke Clara up, and waved at her. Other giant mice then ran on, and they also waved to Clara. Some of the mice skipped around stage, others looked like they were putting on makeup or playing with the presents under the Christmas tree. One mouse actually tapped Clara on the shoulder from behind, and broke into loud laughter as he or she scared her.

Gina liked these antics, and appreciated that ballet could be funny as well as serious. This was so different from her ballet class, which was always so serious. For a moment, Gina wondered how many other ballets had funny moments.

Before she could think this through further, the stage began to change. All the living room furniture and tree disappeared, and were replaced by tall pine trees which were covered in soft white snow. A curtain at the back of the stage lifted, and behind it was a beautiful winter wonderland, including a full moon. Different lights turned on stage, causing the trees to sparkle.

"Magical" Gina thought.

The ballet's famous snow scene started with a few dancers in white tutus running through this landscape, eventually joined by ranks of other snowflakes. Gina realized that many of the steps she saw were the same ones that she and her friends also did in Miss Angelica's production. As a result, her feet began automatically tracing the same patterns under the seat as she sat in the darkened theater watching. She noted that dancers representing the rows of snow were very unified.

They've been rehearsed well. We should try to be this good.

Act I finished with the Nutcracker soldier, triumphant from his victory over the mice and their king, pushing Clara through this winter forest on the sleigh. The curtain lowered just as they reached the snowy trees on the other side.

"That was beautiful" Gina said to Alana.

"I agree, should we get some water and look for your friends?"

Gina hesitated on account of her dress, but the only alternative was to sit there next to the silent Viola. Weighing out the options, Gina decided she'd rather hold the pesky sash rather than feel the awkward bubble surrounding seat 28.

"Sure" Gina replied, standing and gathering up the sash remnants.

"Thomas?"

"No, I'll stay."

Gina and Alana began to inch their way through the aisle, and only when they were a few seats beyond their own did Gina realize she was being closely followed. She turned, and saw Viola right behind her.

"I want some water too. Besides, then I won't have to make small talk to my parents about Act I."

Once they cleared their row, Gina asked "didn't you like it?"

"The dancers are really good" was all that Viola offered.

Walking towards the water fountain in the lobby, Gina spotted Lottie and Viv standing nearby and waved to them. Gina saw both of them stiffen when they saw Viola alongside her.

Oh god.

Before they reached the wary duo, Miss Angelica's arm reached out through the crowd and snared Viola like an octopus tentacle.

"Viola, come tell us what you thought!" she said excitedly.

Viola's body language was the opposite of excited; in fact, she looked suddenly wooden as she was pulled across the short expanse to where Miss Angelica stood with Mr. Stone.

Gina continued to the water fountain, where instead of asking her how she liked Act I, Viv asked "Why were you with Viola?"

"She's sitting next to me, and got up when we got up. I can't help who's sitting where and who wants water" Gina said, frustrated that this resolved issue seemed to be unresolved again.

"Well, she looks as unhappy as ever."

All three girls looked over to where Viola had been hauled to, and saw that her parents had apparently also got up, and all five of them were now standing together in a clump.

"They have to be sisters" Viv said in reference to the resemblance to Miss Angelica and Viola's mom.

"But no one's ever said anything, like it's some sort of secret" Lottie added.

"Maybe they have, and we just weren't in on it" Gina replied to both of them.

"No, I've never heard anyone talk about it at the school" Viv said back.

"Whatever" Gina said turning her back on the Viola mystery. "What did you think of Act I?"

Gina leaned in to drink some water, and detected a slight pause from both her friends who realized that she had tactfully changed the subject from the gossip.

"It was good" Lottie said surrendering to the new topic at hand.

"Viv?"

"I thought the dancing was excellent; it made me look forward to our own show."

"Me too" Gina admitted happily.

"Some of the snow steps are the same as ours" Viv added, sliding back into friendship mold.

"Yeah, but they look a whole lot better" Lottie said eyeing the crowd. "Gina did you see Jake?"

"Yeah, for a second. He didn't see me."

"He looks great tonight. If he goes to Barnums afterwards, you should find some time with him" Lottie continued, still seeing if she could spot him somewhere.

"Girls, we should head back in" Alana said leaning in from a conversation with Lottie's mom.

As though on cue in response to Alana's words, the lights began to go on and off. The mob in the lobby converged.

"Oh…wait, I forgot to tell you guys…Mr. Stone said we can come backstage after the show, let's meet down in front of the orchestra pit right after" Gina said as she was absorbed by the horde filing back into the theater." She waited to hear a response, but didn't hear anything back.

I hope they heard me.

Climbing back into her row, Gina noticed that Viola was sitting again in her seat. Gina hesitated as she felt that she probably should make some kind of small talk until the new act began, but the idea of this felt unnatural to her. But it was also awkward to just sit down and then sit in silence until the lights went out, especially since the seats were so close together.

Silence.

"What did you think of Act I?"

Viola's shoulders slumped as she realized Gina was trying to make conversation.

"I appreciated the dancing; the dancers are good."

"I agree!" Gina said almost too enthusiastically, relieved that Viola actually answered her. "Mr. Stone said we can go backstage afterwards, are you going?"

More silence. Viola did a small sharp head drop of resignation. She turned to face Gina squarely.

"Do you think this is my first ballet, or tenth, or twentieth? Look Gina, yes, I can also go backstage, but not everyone feels the same way you do." Viola hesitated, then continued "I think you should go back and take it all in, because I know it's something that's really special to you. It's just not that way for me."

Before Gina could help herself, she simply asked "then why do you do it?"

"There's a lot you don't know. Like I said, I'm glad you can go backstage. Everyone should be able to chase their dreams."

And with that Gina watched Viola open up and bury her focus into the program she knew she had already read, signaling the conversation's finished.

Gina felt the lights of the theatre dimming to dark and thought this perfectly echoed Viola shutting down

Act II's Land of the Sweets was brought into vivid display with huge cupcakes and cakes piled high with sprinkles lining the sides and back of the stage. Bright orange, red and green candies balanced on top of each other were stacked in piles in-between the baked goods as scenery. Large ice cream cones bordered each wing where the dancers would enter and exit. It was like Barnums had come to the Grand Palace.

This sight made Gina feel happy. Who wouldn't like a kingdom with all these sweets? She sat and appreciated all the various acts of chocolate, tea and assorted goodies, eagerly waiting for the Dew Drop, as well as for Rosalie and Logan to dance the Sugar Plum duet. These were the biggest dance roles in the ballet, and Gina looked forward to seeing these professionals tackle the roles.

Gina sat forward when the Waltz of the Flowers began, and saw that this production did not have individual flowers like their own production. Instead, all the flowers were in the same costume; lime green bodices with long pink tulle tutus. Though they were all alike, Gina had to admit they were beautiful. The Dew Drop entered shortly after, sparkling in a pale turquoise costume that sparkled with many rhinestones sewn on. Gina saw her hair also glimmered in the light and realized she must have put more rhinestones somehow into her hair.

She's beautiful.

The Dew Drop darted, flew, and turned her way through endless patterns the flowers made. Gina was inspired by the shimmering and bold attack she blazed through.

Mr. Stone was right; her confidence and attack are everything. Even if she fell, I would still admire her for her passion.

Gina applauded heartily at the end of the flowers, and sat back seeing Rosalie and Logan enter with the beautiful melody of the Sugar Plum music. Rosalie looked so elegant in a lilac tutu, executing long sustained adagio movements that Gina had always loved to do herself. Logan lifted and partnered her expertly. He also looked dashing in the dark velvet plum jacket he wore.

They looked, and were stunning.

They effortlessly danced the same steps that Gina had been learning all along in her ballet classes with Miss Angelica. This familiarity supported Gina's resolve to keep working so she could perhaps be just like Rosalie.

I already know these steps. I just have to get better at them.

They finished by doing a spectacular last lift in which Logan threw Rosalie high into the air, only to catch her across his body letting go of his hands. It seemed like she was just plastered across him glued like Velcro. In response, many audience members, including Gina, shouted bravo accompanied by furious applause. Gina felt the rush of adrenaline after their successful dance, furthering her resolve to be in their shoes one day.

As the ballet concluded once again back into the Stahlbaum living room with Clara back on the couch, Gina reluctantly knew the ballet was coming to an end. When the final curtain came down, she knew without a shred of doubt that this was what she wanted to do with her life. She joined the audience clapping for all the dancers who were taking their bows, hoping she would someday be the one receiving this type of recognition.

When the last dancers exited the stage, Mr. Stone came back out unexpectedly.

"Hello again. I would like to thank you once again for coming to see our production of The Nutcracker. I hope you enjoyed it as much as we enjoyed dancing it for you. We hope to see you again in the near future when we are back to perform our beloved Swan Lake next year. Until then, have a wonderful holiday and happy new year."

"Swan Lake, what a great way to end the night" Gina said to Alana as they rose from their seats.

Gina turned to say goodbye to Viola, but she was already going out the other way. Gina wondered if she would be backstage despite her negative reaction about it.

Walking out of the row, Thomas turned left as though to leave the theater until Gina tugged at his elbow.

"Dad, we're going backstage, remember?"

Thomas looked impatient, but reluctantly halted and followed Gina and Alana making their way against the crowd to the front of the orchestra pit.

They waited for the others, but no one came.

"They didn't hear me" Gina realized when the theater was mostly emptied out. Not wanting to miss the invitation, Gina, Alana and Thomas found the side door entrance to backstage, and immediately ran into Rosalie taking off her shoes right there in the wings.

"Finally!" Gina heard her say. "These shoes were killing me tonight."

Gina cautiously approached Rosalie, who was sitting right there on the bare floor.

"Oh, hello" Rosalie said looking up.

"Hi" Gina said. "You were beautiful tonight."

"Did you have onions today?" Logan Stark said from somewhere, hidden behind the ice cream scenery, not seeing the small crowd around Rosalie.

"Yep, I sure did. That leftover pizza from…what was the name, Papa something or other. Best pizza I've had in a long time."

"Lou's" Gina replied.

"What?"

"Papa Lou's, that's the name of the pizza place you're talking about."

"Oh. Papa Lou's" Rosalie hollered to Logan. "What's your name?" Rosalie said, rubbing her now released toes.

"Gina. Gina Peabody."

"Nice to meet you Gina Peabody."

Rosalie stood to shake Gina's hand, patting her tutu like someone who pats their sweater after sitting down.

"You too" Gina said, eagerly shaking the hand, despite that it had just rubbed sweaty toes.

Rosalie looked beyond Gina, making Gina realize that in the moment she had forgotten about Alana and Thomas.

"Oh, these are my parents" she said gesturing, but not exactly looking backwards.

"Nice to meet you" Alana said from behind.

"Where do you want to go tonight?" Logan asked, appearing from some dim part of the stage. "Oh, I didn't realize we had company!"

"Logan, this is Gina Peabody, and her parents."

Gina peeled her eyes away from Rosalie, and looked at the very handsome face of Logan, though he seemed a bit sweaty.

After he shook all of their hands, Rosalie broke in and asked "Do you study ballet?"

"Yes, I'm at Miss Angelica's Ballet Academy."

"Oh! So we're dancing with you this next week!"

"Yes! We're super excited, especially after seeing you tonight."

"And what parts are you dancing?"

"Snow, and Daffodil; we have different flowers in our production. I also am the understudy for Dew Drop."

Rosalie smiled "I was the understudy for so many parts for so many years. It gave me time to work out my kinks, so that when I got my first big role, I felt ready."

"That's good to know; I have so many kinks!"

"Ahh, so you've met Rosalie and Logan" Mr. Stone said coming in to the conversation. "I saw this young lady dance earlier this week; she's one to watch" he said smiling down at Gina.

"Well, I look forward to seeing you myself" Rosalie said reaching down to gather up her things.

"Nice to meet you all" Logan said making his way into the dark cavern of backstage.

"Yes, nice to meet you, thank you for coming to our show tonight" Rosalie said turning to follow Logan.

"Oh, you're welcome!" Gina said.

Once she was out of earshot, Gina turned to Alana and then to Mr. Stone, and asked "Why would she thank us? We should be thanking her!"

Mr. Stone answered "because we're appreciative that people come to support us."

"Oh" Gina said, not really getting it, but agreeing nonetheless.

"Have you seen Angelica?" Mr. Stone asked.

Gina heard Alana answer "no," and thought it was strange to hear her name as just Angelica. She was Miss Angelica to almost all who knew her.

"We haven't seen her since the intermission" Alana replied.

"Maybe she's still in the lobby somewhere talking to the audience members" Eric said as he began to back away. "I'm going to go find her."

"Thank you for letting us come backstage" Gina said before he could leave.

"You're very welcome. I'll see you all next week."

Eric smiled and left before abruptly stopping and turning to face the Peabodys.

"Keep working hard Gina" he added, before turning again.

When he was gone and they were alone in the abandoned backstage, Gina crept to the edge of the stage and walked on, looking out to the red velvet seats that had held so many people just a short while ago. Beholding the expanse, she wondered how Rosalie and Logan had felt just a short while ago. The idea of having so many eyes glued on you was both scary and thrilling at the same time. She took a spin in the center, and then walked back to Alana and Thomas who were watching her fantasy from the wings.

"Ready?" Thomas asked.

"Yes."

The three made their way out to join the rest at Barnums.

Chapter Twenty-Four

"Gina, where've you been?" Lottie asked over the noise of Barnums. "We've been here for at least half an hour already."

"We went backstage."

"What?"

"Mr. Stone told me that we could go backstage during intermission. I yelled to you and Viv, but didn't hear you answer back."

"Oh my god, you're kidding!"

"No, for real."

"I can't believe you went back without us!"

"I tried to tell you, but you didn't hear me, and there wasn't time when the lights were flashing to find you."

"And your parent's cell phones weren't working to call us afterwards?"

Gina realized she overlooked a simple way to let Lottie and Viv know to come back.

"I'm so sorry, I didn't think" she said honestly.

"Oh, there you are" Viv said joining them.

"Gina went backstage!" Lottie said accusingly to Viv.

"What?"

"Okay, okay, yes, Mr. Stone caught me just after intermission saying we could go back, but I didn't have time to let you guys know" Gina tried to explain again.

"And apparently didn't think to let us know after either" Lottie said, her head rocking with each word of the sentence.

"I'm really sorry guys, I did yell it out, but then the performance was over, you were gone, and we wanted to get backstage while some of the dancers might still be there."

"And were they?" Viv said somewhat interested.

"Yes! Both Rosalie and Logan!"

"Really?" Viv asked now more interested. Lottie looked even more upset with this revelation. "Was Logan just as handsome up close?"

"Really handsome" Gina gushed. "Except he was pretty sweaty."

"Ugh, I can't believe we didn't hear you." Viv said whining. Gina saw Viv look over to Lottie for her reaction, but Lottie remained silent and looked stony. "Oh, come on Lottie, she wouldn't do it on purpose."

"No, I didn't" Gina said pleadingly.

"How handsome?" Lottie finally said.

"Very" Gina said cracking a smile.

"Next time call us!" Lottie said grabbing and shaking Gina.

Gina shook her head in agreement, and then looked around at all the sweets in glass jars everywhere to be seen. Jars of red and black licorice, big swirly lollypops in rainbows of colors, jelly beans in every shade of red, blue, green, yellow, purple, pink and black, milk chocolate candies, dark chocolate candies, white chocolate candies, candies that looked like real-life fruit and candies made to look like different animals, insects and flowers. Everywhere you looked screamed sugar. And that didn't even count the many flavors of ice cream and cupcakes that also were displayed on all the front counters.

"Our own personal land of the sweets!" Gina said to her friends. "Let's order."

Surrounded by all the choices, Gina settled on a classic hot fudge sundae made with chocolate chip ice cream. Once she had ordered, Lottie basically pushed her out of the way to order a banana split, followed by Viv getting a hot fudge sundae as well.

Gina pried Lottie's fingers off the counter, and moved them over to the side so Alana could order and pay.

"Where's your dad?" Lottie asked rubbing her fingers.

"He's holding a table. Mom must be ordering something for him" Gina said scanning the busy room looking for Thomas. As she looked around, she spotted Jake and his family sitting off in a corner.

"Jake's here" she said turning to her friends.

"Are you going to talk to him?" Viv asked excitedly.

"If he comes over, sure" Gina answered.

"Why don't you just go over there?" Lottie asked.

"That would be weird."

Gina looked back at Jake, and at the same moment he looked over the room and saw her. They both held each other's glance for a second longer than normal until he smiled and waved. Gina felt butterflies in her stomach, and waved back.

"You're blushing!" Lottie leaned in to say to Gina.

"Stop!"

Gina knew she was blushing, and was glad the place was so crowded that no one was probably paying attention to see her face turn all shades of red.

"You can have him, I'll take Logan!" Viv said watching their orders being finished up behind the counter. "Actually, our server's kind of cute" she added, taking a more in depth look of the young man behind the counter.

The alleged cute ice cream builder completed their order and placed too good to be true looking bowls on the counter. Gina picked hers up, and wandered through the obstacle course of the restaurant to find Thomas at their table.

When they were all assembled and digging in, Gina's eyes closed as the velvet smooth warm fudge made its way from the spoon to her stomach. There was no sound for the moment, except for the clinking of spoons against glass.

"Gina, what was Rosalie like?" Viv asked, not looking away from her own bowl.

"She was…normal."

"What do you mean?"

"She was like anyone else, but just in a tutu I guess. I mean, she talked about Papa Lou's, and her toes hurting her. She did say she was an understudy a lot; that seemed good to hear."

"Hi Gina."

Gina looked up to see Jake standing by the table.

When did he sneak up?

"Hi Jake" Gina said looking up. Her gaze was immediately diverted to Lottie, whose eyes had widened at something. Not understanding, Gina saw Lottie quickly run her fingers across her teeth. Gina tilted her head in question quickly at Lottie, who bared her teeth like a cat hissing.

"Fudge" Lottie silently mouthed.

Gina realized she must have fudge smeared across her teeth. *Oh god, first my dress and now brown teeth, great.*

Gina closed her mouth and ran her tongue across all her teeth and indeed tasted a lot of gooey sauce.

"You're good" Jake said smiling, sensing Gina's attempt at becoming presentable.

"So's my sundae apparently" Gina said in return.

"Mine was really good too" he said back. "I saw you and just wanted to say hi."

Not knowing what to say back in front of the rest, Gina sat awkward for a silent second before Alana asked "did Amanda like the performance?"

"A lot, she couldn't sit still the whole night."

"Did you like it?" Gina asked, feeling mature finding something to say.

"Parts, but it was a little long" Jake answered.

"He's honest" Gina thought. "He gets a point for that."

"I should get back, see you later" he said disappearing as quickly as he came.

Gina saw everyone looking at her, and felt self-conscious. She turned her attention to scraping the last remnants of sundae from the sides of the bowl finishing up her dessert. She looked up, and saw everyone still looking at her.

"Well?" Viv asked.

"Well what?"

"Are you glad?"

"He was just being nice."

"Um hmm" Viv chided.

"Are we ready to go home?" Thomas asked, saving Gina.

Everyone nodded, pushing their chairs out.

Chapter Twenty-Five

"Gina, did you get Rosalie's autograph?" Lottie asked sitting in the dark car on the way to the Peabody house.

"I completely forgot."

"We can get them this week" Viv said back.

"Maybe we can get a picture with her" Lottie said.

"Especially one with her in costume; it was so pretty up close" Gina added.

"But what will she do when she no longer wears a tutu?" Thomas suddenly said from the driver's seat.

"What?" Gina answered to the back of his head.

"She was really beautiful tonight; I'll give you that. But I can't help but wondering, what will she do when she's no longer able to do The Nutcracker?"

"Dad, why would you ask that?"

"What? I'm just asking" he responded, after a less than friendly push from Alana sitting next to him in the front seat.

Gina felt uncomfortable with this new line of conversation, especially in front of her friends. Luckily, Viv came to her rescue.

"Well, actually, there's a lot she could do" Gina heard her smart friend say in response to Thomas's question.

Seeing Thomas look back in the rearview, Gina was heartened when Viv continued. "Her career in ballet will have given her great focus on detail; when you learn choreography, you have, HAVE to be precise or the structure of the dance falls apart. She will also be incredibly determined, unafraid to appear in front of people and have a strong sense of commitment. Those skills are ones I'm counting on myself because I know I probably won't have a career in dance like Gina or Lottie, but I know whatever career I *do* go into will be supported by those strengths."

Taking Viv's lead, Gina then continued. "Dad, if Rosalie goes back to school, or if anyone in ballet wants another job after dance, then a lot is possible. After performing, and with the right education, many options are possible. Ballet needs well trained dance teachers who might have gotten a business degree to open their own schools or teach in a university.

Realizing she had a good argument going, Gina ran with this idea, surprising herself with the information that came tumbling out. "Actually, ballet also needs strong women who can run companies like Mr. Stone. I would think that a ballerina who spends many years in the field or maybe even gets a college education could run a ballet company just as good as a man can, or be a manager of a company running lots of things. Ballerinas also would be great physical therapists because we already work with our muscles."

Gina noticed Thomas didn't say anything back, which could be a good thing or a bad thing.

"Dad, we don't just put on tutus and put our hair up in a bun."

Gina waited, but heard Alana speak instead.

"Gina and Viv have good points."

Thomas again said nothing, but Gina took that as a victory.

Score.

Arriving home, the gang came through the garage door and immediately smelled fresh cookies. Gina inhaled the wonderful homey scent, but was too stuffed from Barnums to consider eating anything.

Walking through the house, they looked for Miss Bea so that they could tell her about the show. Seeing her in the living room, the girls rushed in.

Bea Bumble was reading quietly in a big overstuffed chair when the girls pounced in. Looking up, she raised her finger to her lips "the little one fell asleep right here on the sofa."

Gina looked over and saw Benny sleeping on the couch under a blanket Miss Bea had placed on him.

"He made a cookie just for you" Miss Bea whispered. "It's round, and pretty lopsided, but he said it looked like your ballet hairdo."

Thomas went over and gently picked up Benny to carry him to his room. As Thomas lifted him, Benny half woke up and said sleepily "Hi Gina, how was the bullay?"

"It was really good" Gina quietly replied.

Gina watched Thomas carry Benny away, and as soon as he disappeared, she descended on Miss Bea and began to talk about the events of the night.

"Oh, my goodness" Miss Bea declared, leaning in to the girls. "This seems like way too much to hear about this late. Why don't the three of you come over to my house sometime in the next few days and tell me every last detail!"

Gina smiled at the thought of a cozy afternoon at Miss Bea's house; no doubt more cookies could play into this scenario.

"Goodnight girls" she said standing up.

Gina heard Alana thanking Miss Bea, and then asking Thomas to blow up the air mattresses.

"We're so lucky to have her as a neighbor" Gina said to her friends as they walked down the hall and up towards Gina's bedroom. Getting into her comfy pajamas, Gina said "thanks Viv for giving my dad all that great information."

"No problem. I had the same conversation with my parents a year ago. I wish everyone understood that ballet wasn't just something frilly."

"My parents don't even ask, they just let me do whatever" Lottie added.

"Oh, I think mom and dad will always let me" Gina responded, "but dad always downplays ballet as something I'll grow out of."

"As in…he still won't let you go to New York?" Viv asked.

"I don't know, we haven't talked about it, but at least I've gotten in some good ammo towards the idea." Looking up from zipping up a zipper, Gina added "with your help as well."

Gina led them back out, and stopped when they reached the family room and looked in. All the lights in the room had been turned off, and strands of twinkling white and colored lights had been hung all around the area where Thomas had placed the air mattresses. It looked like they would be sleeping underneath a fairy tale sky.

"Oh Mom, it's beautiful!" Gina said quietly, her eyes delighted by the enchanted setting.

"We thought you would like it" Alana said softly.

"And look" Lottie exclaimed running to the window, "it's snowing outside." They all ran to look as this was very rare where they lived.

"Just like the ballet" Gina thought, imagining the snowflakes as ballerinas cascading across the heavens in the winter sky.

Gina looked over at Alana and Thomas watching her, and was filled with gratitude. Without saying a word, she went over and gave them each a big hug.

Breaking away, Gina, scrambled over to get into her bed under the covers, and watched as Lottie and Viv joined her happily getting into their own snug spaces.

Gina had barely slid her legs into her inviting bed, when she felt a large lump come from behind.

"OH NO! Stella! Gina shouted at the dog, there's not enough room for you and me in this bed!"

Stella was determined to sleep with Gina, and tried desperately to get into the small space alongside Gina.

"Oh alright, I just won't be able to move at all!" Gina said reluctantly.

Gina laid quietly for a second, and then sat up propped on her elbows.

"Wouldn't it be awesome if when we grew up, we all lived together in New York?"

"I actually thought that a few days ago" Lottie said.

Gina noticed Viv was quiet, and for a moment thought maybe she had fallen asleep.

"What do you think Viv?"

In the semi-dark of the room, Viv replied after a short moment "I would love that, but in all reality, I don't know if it will ever happen for me."

"What do you mean?" Gina said sitting up.

"You and Lottie have a good shot at making it in the ballet world. Gina, you're so graceful, and Lottie, you're a spitfire. I don't have any of those qualities, and like I said to your dad earlier, I probably will use dance for something, but that something probably won't involve dancing in a company."

Gina knew Viv struggled with her flat feet in a field that demanded arches. She wanted to say something like "that's not true," but she knew that Viv was too smart to buy it. Instead, she said something more honest, and more valuable.

"You don't have to dance to live in New York. Whatever you do land up doing, you could do it there even if both Lottie and I are dancing in some company there, and even if none of us is dancing in a company there. We should just stick together."

"Thanks Gina" Viv said, settling deeper into her covers.

Gina laid back down, and began to think of the week ahead. As she fought off sleep for a second to imagine the events, she felt happy and nervous at the same time. So much that she wanted in life was literally just a long arm reach in front of her. She felt she had a really good chance of getting one of the scholarships. It was really, really close. Actually, by this time next week they might know. But what if her instincts were off? What if she was setting herself up for some huge disappointment? She was about to bring up the subject, but stopped because she didn't want to hurt Viv's feelings by talking about something that she and Lottie alone might only enjoy.

Instead, she switched gears. "Can we talk about how bad my dress looked by the end of the night?"

Waiting to hear her friends giggle at the thought of this, Gina realized it was suddenly quiet. Too quiet. Gina glanced over and saw that both of her friends had fallen asleep in the short few minutes she had pondered about the end of the week.

Gina smiled at her sleeping friends and turned to look up at the twinkling white lights. As her own eyes started to get heavy, Gina thought about Rosalie, and how much she had impressed her both on and off the stage.

In the hush of the winter night, Gina snuggled into her covers.

I've just got to dance my best.

Chapter Twenty-Six

Gina was inspired and full of energy when she arrived at the ballet studios the following Monday. They would only be doing run-throughs of the ballet from now on, finishing with a dress rehearsal on Thursday night at their local high school theater. Though it wasn't as beautiful as The Grand Palace, it still held the promise of something special.

The first part of the week flew by quickly. Each passing day brought the level of anticipation up a notch. Gina felt it, and responded with good power and attack. Miss Angelica complimented her, Miss Monopoly said nothing. Viola looked sullen each day, but that was nothing new.

On Wednesday, Rosalie and Logan arrived to block out their parts in Miss Angelica's version. Once again, Gina was taken aback, not in a bad way, by how ordinary they acted and seemed in real life. She had expected them to be regal in some way, but found that she admired them even more by realizing that they were just people who happened to put on nice costumes and look beautiful on stage. This made it seem like it could happen for anyone, even her.

Gina noticed that Rosalie had a puzzled look on her face watching Viola's Dew Drop. Though her dancing was very clean without a single flaw, Gina wondered if Rosalie was tuned into the fact that Viola didn't look happy. Gina kept watching Rosalie, and eventually saw her whisper something to Miss Monopoly who was seated right next to her. Miss Monopoly's face immediately hardened just slightly, enough to signal to Gina that she was displeased.

When the run-through was over, Rosalie was generous in offering to give a last-minute pep talk to the entire cast. As everyone gathered around her and Logan, they each took a turn to talk about what an extraordinary opportunity they had before them. They talked about their own individual rises within the ranks of The National Ballet, along with some really funny stories of mishaps and falls. The entire group laughed listening to Rosalie joke about how badly she had fallen, or Logan forgetting the choreography on stage in his early years. Their lightheartedness put everyone at ease this close to the show.

When they wished everyone a good night's sleep, Gina was ready to go until she heard Miss Angelica thank everyone for their hard work, but that Miss Monopoly would like to go through Dew Drop again in the upstairs studio. Everyone else was excused.

"Tell my mom that I will be done in a bit if you see her in the parking lot" Gina said to Lottie and Viv. She picked up her bag with slight dread. She didn't mind the extra rehearsal, in fact, she hoped she might get a chance to do it and that maybe Rosalie and Logan might stick around to see her dance. She dreaded the idea that Miss Monopoly was obviously mad or unhappy with something, most likely from whatever Rosalie whispered to her. If she was mad, then there was no telling what might happen upstairs.

Gina entered the deserted studio upstairs, and could tell Viola was displeased by the way she entered and threw her bag down. If she was unhappy, she didn't say anything (no surprise), but her body language told Gina that she didn't want to be there.

Like a strong gust from an incoming storm, Miss Monopoly whooshed in and shut the door behind her. Gina watched her walk silently over to the sound system to load her music in, and then turned to face them.

As if they were just starting the day rather than finishing it, she evenly said "from the top Viola."

Gina looked over to Viola who stood motionless for just a second too long, and then walked to the center of the room for the beginning pose of Dew Drop. Gina felt tension surrounding all of them.

Viola had only gotten through a few phrases when Miss Monopoly stopped the music like ripping off a band-aid. Gina sensed she had just been marking time before she could let loose.

"Viola! Exactly what kind of school do you think we are?" she said, her arms doing some kind of scolding macabre choreography before landing in a resting place expertly placed on her hips.

Only Gina's eyes moved to hear a response, but Viola stood silent. Gina realized it almost looked like she was standing her ground against the mighty will of Miss Monopoly.

Gina waited for either of the two to speak, suspecting that she was a forgotten entity that somehow was present and witness to this brewing eruption.

Miss Monopoly broke the silent vise by answering her own question. "I'll tell you what kind of school we are. We are a school of integrity. A school that works hard, HARD at making sure every detail and every aspect of what we produce from the studio to the stage is as polished and professional as possible."

Gina noted that her eyes were becoming narrower and narrower in tandem with her voice rising in volume.

"Do you know why I stopped the music, or why I bothered to stay late and rehearse this part on my own time again?" Gina heard, and saw that her eyes now were just slits boring into Viola.

"I suppose because you wanted to yell at me" Gina shockingly heard Viola say back.

Miss Monopoly seemed to fill with some kind of invisible air pump; her shoulders rose so high she didn't seem to have a neck anymore.

"YOU UNGRATEFUL CHILD!" she yelled out. "You've been given every, EVERY opportunity that most dancers would kill for, and you respond with utter lack of interest and appreciation!" Without looking at Gina, Miss Monopoly began to walk small circles around Viola, like a predator about to strike in for a kill.

"Do you know what Rosalie whispered to me during rehearsal?" she asked as her circles slowed up.

Gina knew the question was not a question, as she was just pausing before revealing the answer.

"She wanted to know if you were bored." "BORED!" "As if we were amateurs who didn't know how to cast the roles!"

Gina had now blended herself into the wall as best she could, hoping to stay unnoticed while this argument continued.

"I didn't ask to be cast!" Viola yelled back.

Miss Monopoly, who was now red in addition to virtually having no eyes left at all, seemed to weigh her next move carefully.

Gina watched her choose just the right works, before leaning forward and asking "And what would your mother think of all of this?" Gina saw her arms had resumed their dance of madness, as they swirled around in the air in response to Viola's obvious defiance.

"She wouldn't realize, just like she never has."

Gina waited for more information to come out, but neither Viola or Miss Monopoly said anything for a few seconds.

Gina felt the spotlight on her as Miss Monopoly pointed her way and said "I have half a mind to replace you with Gina, and pray she doesn't fall."

"You should! She actually WANTS to dance it!" Viola half screamed; half pleaded.

"I'm done with trying to reason with you!" Miss Monopoly said and turned to walk back to the sound system. "And I'm done wasting my time" she continued, as she pushed the slot to remove her music.

Gina watched her put the music away and pick up her bag. She turned to Viola one last time to say "I suggest you think about what all of this would mean to your mother. And I suggest you think long and hard about New York, and what THAT would mean to your mother if you didn't get one of the summer slots." She took one sad look at Viola, and walked out the door without bothering to close it behind her.

Gina still stood frozen to the wall in back, not knowing what to say or do. It was so awkward. She wanted to console Viola, but didn't know what had happened, or if Viola even wanted to be consoled.

She thought it might be a moot point, as Viola went back to her things and appeared to pack up. Gina freed herself from her support wall, and was about to get her own things, when she saw

Viola suddenly and swiftly pick up one of her pointe shoes and throw it with all her might at the sound system.

"Viola!"

Gina watched Viola pick up her other shoe and throw it even harder at the system. Though it missed, it did connect with a glass vase sitting near it, and shattered it all over the floor.

Viola picked up her whole bag and threw it forward in a fit of rage that Gina had never seen before. Gina didn't know what was more shocking; the actual fit or Viola actually showing some kind of emotion.

"Nobody understands!" she yelled out.

"Understands what?" Gina said coming forward to try to help.

Instead of answering, Gina heard Viola suppress an inner scream, as though whatever demons she was feeling were trapped within her body, unable to vocalize.

"Understands what?" Gina repeated.

As Viola ignored her question with more frustration, Gina tried to walk closer to put her hand on Viola's shoulder in support.

"Stop Gina!, I don't need your help."

"Viola, talk to me!"

"No Gina, it's too complicated!"

"What's complicated?"

Viola said nothing, but Gina could tell she was struggling.

"What's complicated?" Gina repeated yet again. Without thinking, Gina blurted out "that Miss Angelica's your aunt?"

Viola's head shook violently back and forth in response to Gina's suspicion.

'NO, NO, NO Gina" she yelled out. "Miss Angelica's not my aunt! She's my mother!"

Chapter Twenty-Seven

Gina didn't see this piece of the Viola puzzle coming. Sitting quietly on the floor next to the now softly crying Viola, Gina listened as Viola poured out her story:

"My birth mom Angelica Wentworth and my adopted mom Patricia Wentworth have always been very close sisters. They both got accepted into the school of The National Ballet, and then each was invited to join the company, Patricia first, then Angelica. They were really happy.

Before long, it became obvious that the company thought Angelica had more star power, and they began to cast her in some big major roles. Patricia was happy to dance on the sidelines, and supported Angelica as she rose up the ladder to success.

After a few years, Angelica was promoted to principal status, and began dating a guy in the company. Patricia had also met a young man, but the two men were very different from each other.

James Barkus was an up and coming New York financial banker when he accepted an invitation from friends to join them at an evening at the ballet. Going to a reception with them afterwards, he spotted Patricia Wentworth and immediately fell in love. From that point on, he came to as many performances as he could, got educated about ballet, and eventually asked Patricia out to dinner. They started seriously seeing one another, and fell in love. Patricia was heartbroken a year later, when James unhappily told her his company had plans to begin a new branch in northern Florida, and that he was being given a huge promotion to run it. He told her he didn't want to leave her, and asked her to marry him. Patricia said yes, though she was scared of leaving her career, New York, and sister behind.

Angelica meanwhile, had caught the eye of a very handsome dancer in the company, who was trouble. He partied a lot, and was seen with many women. Patricia was worried that Angelica would eventually get hurt, but Angelica continued seeing him. After James asked Patricia to marry him, Angelica found out that she was going to have a baby. Angelica was really happy, and hoped that her boyfriend would marry her. Unfortunately, it was the opposite. Apparently, he didn't want to get married, or have a child, and went off the deep end. He began partying every night, drinking, and missing class and rehearsals. He was fired a short time later, and disappeared dancing somewhere in Europe."

Gina saw Viola pause for a second to look at her.

"Neither my real or adopted mom will even tell me his name. I don't even know the name of my real father."

Gina didn't even know how to respond to that fact, and felt that it must be some kind of blank hole Viola carried around. Viola continued:

"The whole company felt sorry for Angelica, who was embarrassed at how this was playing out. One dancer who was especially sympathetic was Eric Stone, aka Mr. Stone. He offered to marry Angelica, but she didn't love him and said no. She started to panic wondering how she was going to raise a baby alone, Patricia leaving, and how she would make ends meet. She knew she was in too deep, and became desperate. Patricia stepped in, and offered that she and James could raise the baby. At first Angelica wouldn't hear of giving up the baby, but once I had been born, she became so overwhelmed and helpless that she sadly let her sister and brother-in-law adopt me.

She returned to the company, and Patricia and James raised me here. Angelica found the company was not the same; while she was gone, others had come in and taken her roles. Angelica was not given the parts back, and began to feel deceived that she could resume her career as before. She didn't regret having me, but regretted the cards she had been dealt. She eventually retired, and wanting to be near me, she moved here and opened a ballet school. Both she and Patricia have set it in their minds that I would be the ballet dancer that each of them never was."

Viola took a deep breath, "it has become their mission to groom me into the ultimate ballet dancer, except nobody has ever, EVER asked me what I want. I don't want this responsibility, this sack tied around my waist. I drag around their hopes and dreams and while I don't want to let either of them down, I also don't have the passion for ballet like they did. I know they each love me, and I actually understand why my real mom gave me to Patricia. But I don't want a career in ballet, and also don't want to hurt either of them. I'm trapped."

As if on an intuitive cue, Gina simply asked "What *DO* you want Viola?"

For a moment, Gina saw Viola confused by her question.

"Gina, I think you're the first, very first person to actually ask me that."

"What's your dream Viola?"

Gina saw Viola's face light up for the first time in her life.

"Gina, I love to sing! And I love musicals. I would love to still perform, but I want to be on Broadway, not in a ballet company. I stay after school some nights when we don't have ballet and take singing lessons with our music teacher at school, and she even works with me some times during lunch. I listen to all the soundtracks of musicals that I can find, and practice them over and over again when I'm alone. "

Gina had never seen Viola so enthused; she looked... *lighter.*

"I would like to hear you sing sometime" Gina offered.

Gina saw Viola didn't know what to say for a second.

"Gina, that means a lot to me, I would love to sing for someone, anyone."

"You're welcome."

After a moment, Gina got up to grab a tissue to give to Viola, who accepted it and blew her nose like she was blowing away all her kept secrets and burdens. In the silence, she looked at Gina and said "Gina, you should be dancing Dew Drop. I can fake injuring my ankle or something tonight or tomorrow, and you can step in and dance your heart out in this role. You've worked just as hard, actually harder with all those theraband exercises you've done over the last month. And you actually want it."

Gina stood motionless.

"You should be doing this part" Viola repeated.

And here it was: the golden opportunity! Gina's mind quickly understood and took in that this was her chance. Her heart kicked up a notch, imagining that she could be wearing that pale blue green costume and dancing the part she had admired for so many years!

Could it happen? The applause? The extra opportunity to be seen, and in something stronger than Daffodil?

Gina's heartbeat continued escalating.

But...

But...

Something seemed wrong. Gina wanted this badly, but another feeling kept intruding on her delicious trance. She realized that she also knew that if she took Viola up on her offer, she would be dancing via a lie. And with this, Gina discovered the maturity of having to say no.

"Viola, you can't do that."

"Why not? I don't want to dance it, and you do. Besides, you'll look beautiful, as long as you remember to put your whole foot down before any of the turns!"

"Because it's a lie. Besides, I think you should dance it."

"Why should I dance it? I just told you I don't want to."

"Because I think you owe it to yourself to know what it feels like. Look Viola, you can dance circles around anyone here at the studio. For what it's worth, for all the pushing you might have received from either of your moms, at least it's paid off. You are one of the strongest dancers here, and even if you quit Friday night after the show, at least you should know what it feels like to do one of the best parts in a ballet. Then you'll never have to look back and wonder what if might have felt like."

"Gina, you do realize that I'm basically handing you this part right now, don't you?"

"I know, but I wasn't picked first, and if you fake an injury, then I'll still always be the default. I want to be the first choice because I'm the one anyone wants."

Gina waited for Viola to respond, but she had nothing to say to that.

Gina continued. "Viola, you need to tell your parents, all of them, including your dad, about your dreams. If they love you as much as you think, then they might be disappointed, but they ultimately would want you to be happy. It might take them some time to readjust, but they would. And if you dance Dew Drop, and dance it with all your heart knowing that it can decide your future, then at least you will be able to point out to them, and more importantly, to yourself, that ballet is not your destiny if you still feel the same way after dancing this amazing part."

This time Gina didn't wait for Viola to say anything because she knew the conversation had no more left to be said. She picked up her things and walked over to the door.

"Gina, you've been a friend, the first one I've had here."

Gina turned around at Viola's words and said "lucky you didn't break the sound system! Can you imagine Monopoly's reaction?"

Chapter Twenty-Eight

Gina woke up early the next day ready for the dress rehearsal. Alana had been proud of her when she told her all about what had happened with Viola on the way home yesterday, and Gina felt good about how she handled it as she laid in bed.

Though Gina dreamed of donning that mint costume, she was happy nonetheless thinking about her Daffodil costume. It was a bright yellow tutu, with long green strands painted up the sides of the costume. Gina thought it was bright and happy, and everyone said it was a good color for her. Getting out of bed, she was determined to make the best of this part.

When Alana dropped her off at the high school theater after school finished, Gina made her way to the dressing room allotted to all the dancers.

As she walked into the ruckus of swarming dancers, she heard "over here Gina," and looked over to see that Lottie and Viv had saved a place for her at a mirror to the right.

"Hi guys" she said as she threw her bag down on the floor under the counter and grabbed the small sack which held her stage makeup.

Gina loved the idea of costumes and make-up; it seemed glamorous to her. Looking through the mirror, she saw the rack of costumes at the rear of the room with her daffodil hung waiting. It made her smile.

As she began to methodically arrange her make-up just so (a superstitious routine!) she tried to chatter with Lottie and Viv above the noise, but it was hard. She had decided that she would not share Viola's story with them just yet because she felt it was too personal, and her inner conscious warned her to respect this.

In the middle of trying to yell out something to Lottie, the room became hushed. Gina looked around to see why everyone had stopped talking, and saw Miss Monopoly standing in the doorway.

"Gina Peabody, can I see you for a moment?"

Gina felt like a magnet as all eyes on the room turned in her direction. Not knowing what Miss Monopoly wanted (it usually did not bode well), Gina got up hesitantly and walked over and out the door to the waiting teacher.

"Gina, you will be doing Dew Drop for this dress rehearsal."

"What?"

"You will be doing Dew Drop."

"What happened to Viola?"

"She is unable to be here today, make sure you're warm and ready" was all Miss Monopoly would explain.

Gina was left in the hall watching Miss Monopoly walk away, and frantically thought about Viola's disappearance.

Did she really fake an injury?

Did she really get injured somehow?

Is she sick?

Gina didn't know what had happened, and couldn't guess why she wasn't here. Her thoughts focused on Dew Drop, and she was suddenly nervous. She slipped back into the dressing room, and was somewhat hidden by all the commotion going on.

"What happened?" Lottie asked.

"I'm doing Dew today."

"What?"

"Viola's not here. Viv, that means you're doing Daffodil."

"Where's Viola?"

"I don't know, Monopoly just told me she wasn't here, and that I'm doing Dew today."

Gina plopped into her chair. This had been a roller-coaster of events. She didn't know what Viola's absence meant, but did know that she was expected now to fill in, and fill in well.

With a rush of adrenaline, Gina realized that if Mr. Stone is here for the dress rehearsal, then he would see her in something better that the daffodil solo. When this thought made its way through her brain, she got even more nervous.

"Gina, you look white" Viv said looking at her.

"I never thought I would actually dance this; you always assume as the understudy you'll just remain someone who learned it in the back."

"This is like a movie" Lottie said, "Maybe you'll get to perform it tomorrow! Gina, you'll rock in the part!"

Gina sat silent putting her make-up on, and tried to concentrate on the fact that this was just a rehearsal, not the real thing. She tried to make random small talk with her friends, but they soon gave up when they saw how preoccupied she was.

Gina finished getting ready, and went to get her snow costume.

At least I have this part first, it should break my nerves.

"Ten minutes till the start of the run" some person Gina didn't recognize called out up and down the hallway.

Gina put on the snow costume, took one last check in the mirror, and followed Lottie and Viv out to go backstage.

Walking into the dark cavern, Gina began to warm up, mentally reminding herself of putting her foot down for the Dew turns coming later. As she went over this correction, she saw Miss Angelica on the other side of the stage talking quietly with Miss Monopoly. Gina noticed that Miss Angelica looked different: her posture was not as straight as usual, and most glaringly, her hair seemed…messy. Not as bad as "unexpectedly caught in a rainstorm messy", but it was not her usual either. Gina spied loose ends pulled out of what was always a glossy lacquered perfection of a hairdo. She guessed her hair aligned somehow with Viola not being here, and felt a sudden sadness for her teacher and for whatever might have happened.

Gina didn't have time to ponder these details for long as the overture music began. Gina watched both teachers exit through a door leading them to the seats in the audience where they would watch the rehearsal.

Here we go.

When Gina heard the music of snow begin, she went into auto-pilot mode and breezed through the dance. There were no snarky turns, balances or other roadblocks to think about, and she did in fact lose some of her nerves by getting on stage first in this tamer section.

Act II was almost a blur. Going back into the dressing room before the second act, Gina went to the costume rack and bypassed the yellow tutu and carefully took out the mint green one instead. Luckily, Viola and she were about the same size, so this would fit her nicely.

Gina put on the tutu, running her hands gently down the sides as though she could feel the unique color and sparkle that it possessed. She felt a thrill just wearing it.

"Gina, it looks wonderful on you" Lottie said behind her.

Gina turned to say thanks, then stepped back to take a second look at her friend.

"Lottie, you also look wonderful, stunning in fact!"

It was true: Gina's eyes took in Lottie, looking gorgeous in the pale pink tutu of the carnation. Her dark hair accented the pale rose color perfectly.

"I clash!"

Gina looked over at Viv, whose red hair did in fact clash with the yellow of the Daffodil tutu.

"Viv, you look…radiant!" Gina offered.

"Thanks, but this is definitely not a good color scheme!"

The sight of Viv's comedically mismatched tones broke any of Gina's remaining nerves. She went and hugged Viv, who had taken her look in stride with good humor.

"You'll definitely stand out!"

This was what Gina thought of right before her entrance for Dew Drop. She looked out and saw both her friends dancing strongly, and this sight filled her with eagerness to join them. She flew out of the wings on her musical cue, and began tracing the patterns and phrases with glorious freedom, occasionally glimpsing the costume float out of the corner of her eye. This only made her more passionate, which was reflected in her genuine and honest smile throughout the solo. She remembered to place her foot correctly, and took off and landed each turn well. When she finished with a giant jump offstage, she almost ran into Rosalie and Logan who were standing in the wing ready for their entrance.

"That was a beautiful job, well done!" Rosalie quickly said before Logan led her away on stage.

Everyone backstage surrounded Gina with compliments and congratulations. She felt on top of the world.
I wonder if Mr. Stone was here to see?

Chapter Twenty-Nine

Gina arrived at the theatre the night of the show ready for anything. Her spin as Dew Drop the night before instilled a new level of confidence for whatever the night would bring.

Alana had been sitting in the theater for the dress rehearsal the night before, and she found Gina backstage after the second Act to rush over to tell her how proud she was of her. Their whole ride home was filled going over every detail of the entire run through, especially focusing on Gina's unexpected turn in this plum part. Mr. Stone had been there after all, and found her after the rehearsal to compliment her.

"Miss Peabody, that was a pleasure to watch. You took my correction about being passionate to heart, and it showed in a remarkable presentation."

This could not have played out better. She felt like she scored a big victory.

Later, Gina was so wound up, that it had been hard for her to fall asleep, but once she did, she slept deeply and was surprised when the alarm sounded the next morning.

Gina had not heard anything more about Voila. In fact, no one seemed to have any information about why she hadn't been there. Even though Gina had discovered Viola's source of unhappiness, and guessed that it factored in somehow as to why she hadn't been there, she ate her breakfast not knowing how or if it might affect the real show tonight.

This thought wove circles around and around in her head all day, exhausting her mind with questions. She asked Alana if they could leave early for the theater, in case anything new had surfaced, one way or another. She wanted to be prepared.

Her answer came quickly; Viola was sitting in the dressing room applying make-up when Gina arrived. Only a few other dancers were there early, and they were engaged in conversations at the other end of the room not paying attention.

"Viola...what happened yesterday, are you okay?"

"It's a long story, but a good one. I'll tell you later if we can find someplace private."

"You didn't fake an injury, or are injured, are you?"

"No, I thought about it, but no. I'll tell you later."

Gina didn't press the issue as more dancers began to filter in, but felt let down somehow. There had been so much excitement; both in a sudden cast change, and the fact that the very cast change had involved her. She would have liked to continue the new set of thrilling events, but things were back to normal. As evidence, the Dew Drop tutu was now hung right behind where Viola was sitting.

Gina went and sat at her own spot, and went through the motions of her make-up routine. Lottie and Viv soon joined her, and Gina almost got annoyed at their cackling. Gina knew she should be excited, this was THE show, but after last night, she simply didn't want to go back to just doing the smaller role. As she thought about this inadvertent demotion, she felt ashamed that she felt this way.

"Good evening ladies!"

Gina turned and saw Miss Angelica and an unusually happy looking Miss Monopoly standing in the doorway.

"We're finally here!" Miss Angelica warmly purred out, clasping her hands together in delight. We are so proud of all of you, and hope that all your work has paid off."

"Yes, and remember all your corrections" Miss Monopoly squeaked out. "You want to dance your best" she trailed off swirling her finger at each of them. As they smiled and turned to leave, Miss Monopoly half-turned back to all of them "Mr. Stone's announcing the summer spots after the show, so again…remember your corrections!"

"What?" Gina said to Lottie and Viv, "he's announcing tonight?"

"I guess so" Lottie replied, surprised as well.

"I thought they would think about it, and let us know in a few days or something!"

"Guess not" Viv added, "and it's just like Monopoly to add a fear factor to try to get us to dance better."

Gina momentarily wished Viola was not there, but then realized that Mr. Stone had seen her dance Dew last night. She would have to be content that she was lucky to have been in that part at all, and would make the most of what she originally was cast to dance. With this resolved in her mind, she, like everyone else, began to feel the adrenaline growing as they all scampered to finish getting ready.

When Gina heard the familiar "10 minutes" till curtain announcement, she also became aware of another noise which always inspired her: the loudspeaker system captured the hustle and bustle noise of the audience entering into the theater. Gina imagined all the people arriving and was filled with more anticipation. Stepping into her Snow costume, she saw Amanda out of the corner of her eye, and knew that Jake was probably one of those people sitting out front.

"Ready guys?" Gina asked trembling with expectation.

"Yes, let it snow!" Lottie sang out.

Gina and her friends exited the dressing room and made their way backstage to watch until the time when the snow section started. As the overture began and the audience quieted, Gina looked around as saw everyone focus and pull themselves together. Gina loved this moment of intense collaboration and community; everyone was ready to make all their individual work shine into one beautiful presentation. Gina loved being a part of something so big.

As the dancers in the first party scene took their places, Gina watched them enter the stage on cue with the music, and it all began. As far as she could tell, all was going really well leading up to the final portion of Act I, the snow scene. Gina took off the sweat pants she had been wearing to keep warm, and took her place in line ready for her own first entrance. She sailed onstage on cue and felt airborne and magical with her white costume flying all around her. She made eye contact with the others in the section, each knowing that they were finally performing and showing off their skills. Gina capitalized on this aspect, filling each of her moves with lush stretches and breathtaking extensions. Though it was an ensemble section, Gina finished feeling satisfied and very happy about her performance.

Gathered back in the dressing room before Act II, Gina and the others were joyful. Multiple conversations about "this moment" and "that moment" converged into one big noisy blob. They were so absorbed in the ruckus that at first, they didn't see or hear Miss Angelica, who had stopped in their doorway with words of praise and encouragement.

"Ladies, ladies....Ladies!"

The room hushed a bit.

"Ladies, that was wonderful!" Gina saw that Miss Angelica was genuinely pleased. "Keep up this good energy for act II! We will all meet onstage afterwards."

Gina smiled and saw Miss Angelica look past all of them to look at Viola for just a second longer than normal. Viola looked back at her, and smiled.

Viola smiled.

She actually smiled!

No one knew their situation, but Gina thought that maybe Viola had come to some kind of determination, one way or another. Since there wasn't any time for her and Viola to talk about what had happened, and since she couldn't talk about it with anyone else, Gina instead walked over and plucked the yellow tutu off the rack.

"Viola looks...beautiful!" Gina heard Lottie say.

Gina turned and saw that Viola had also gotten into her tutu. Her brown hair and pale eyes were set off exquisitely by the pale costume. She looked like a movie star.

"Five minutes!" that unfamiliar voice cried out in the hallway.

The dancers once again filtered out on their way backstage. They swung open the stage door and ran into Rosalie and Logan, who had used the intermission to block out some final moves in the temporarily empty space.

"Dance beautifully everyone!" Rosalie gleefully said. Logan only gave a thumbs up in response.

Passing them in the hall, Gina saw Lottie staring at Logan.

"He's so handsome!" she said seemingly for the 200th time.

"He sure is!" Gina heard behind her, and saw that Viola was following them to the stage. Gina fell back a bit, and quietly asked "you ready?"

"Very" was all Viola replied. Gina didn't know what that meant, but there was no time to discuss it.

Gina and Lottie watched as Viv led her string of little angels in her role as head angel when Act II began. Gina saw that Viv looked mature and tender with the young dancers, and thought she would make a great teacher someday, if she wanted. The rest of the dances that she could watch before Flowers echoed the success of the first act; everyone was dancing their best.

Gina got into place for their entrance, and looked back to give a quick nod to Viola, who entered slightly later than the rest. Gina only was able to see Viola smile back before she was once again vaulting onto the stage.

Gina did the first ensemble phrase, before everyone peels off to expose the individual flower parts. She ran in the wings to watch as Lottie's carnation was the first solo. Gina saw Lottie send a look of daring defiance to gravity and take off for one, two, three, FOUR turns to begin her dance. She had never done that many before! Lottie continued her streak of dynamic strength and skill by flying in her jumps and executing more turns than she had ever done in rehearsal.

She was on fire!

When she exited, Gina rushed over briefly while another solo had their moment.

"That was amazing Lottie!"

"Thanks, I don't know how I pulled that off, but it was so fun!"

Gina smiled, and then it was time for her own daffodil solo. Gina knew this part by heart. When she entered the stage however, she momentarily thought of Lottie's death defying turn just a moment ago, and compared it to the blander choreography she was presently doing. As such, for a moment she felt out of her own body, and not fully engaged in her part. Luckily, she caught herself thinking in a split second, and continued as usual until the end. When she got off stage, she felt insecure about how she did, and found Viv standing there.

"Was that okay?"

"What do you mean?"

"I might have lost concentration for a second."

"I didn't notice."

"Really?"

"Really."

Gina relaxed, as she knew Viv always told the truth. Or at least she hoped she did. She turned her attention back to the stage as it was time for the Dew Drop solo, and she wanted to see how Viola would do.

The minute Viola stepped on stage, Gina was mesmerized. Gone was the robotic indifference, replaced instead with radiant emotion that was expressed with genuine warmth, smiles and luminous glances. She had always been a skilled technician, now she looked like a complete artist.

"Wow" Gina murmured watching Viola sweep through all the routines they had done alone together under Miss Monopoly's ruthless watch.

Viola held balances flirting with the music, jumped as though her life depended on it, and expertly landed each and every turn like a professional. She was striking.

Because she didn't have any friends among the dancers, no one felt comfortable approaching her after her solo to congratulate her. Gina boldly walked over when they were all finished.

"You were just stunning."

"Thanks Gina."

Gina felt this was enough, and for a moment, thought that Viola might cry. To spare her any embarrassment, she and the others watched Rosalie and Logan who had now entered for their portion of the ballet.

All the dancers stood silently to view the two professionals who exceeded their expectations. They capped off the ballet gloriously with their duet. The audience exploded with applause when they finished leading to the finale.

Gina and the other dancers also clapped from the wings. Gina again knew without a shadow of a doubt that she wanted to be Rosalie one day. As Rosalie and Logan slowly walked off stage, Gina passed them on her way out for the finale. She wanted to reach out and touch them, but hesitated being so personal. In some ways it was hard to have an idol so close. On one hand, you want to be a part of their existence, but on the other hand, you don't want to intrude and spoil any connection. As Gina waltzed out for the finale, eventually joined by the two stars, she had a sudden jolt of satisfaction knowing the connection was there by way of this ballet. She used that motivation to propel her through the last bits of the performance.

Chapter Thirty

And then, just like that, it was over. Gina stood in line for her bows, taking in the praise of bravos hurling from the audience. When the final curtain came down, the stage erupted with shouts of cheers all around. Everyone was hugging everyone with greetings of "well done" repeated over and over again. Gina made her rounds and saw Miss Angelica, Miss Monopoly, Mr. Black and Mr. Stone arriving in a grand entrance flashing smiles to all.

The crowd of dancers quieted immediately in anticipation for what they might say.

"Dancers, I'm so, so immensely proud of each and every one of you" Miss Angelica led off.

"Well done" Mr. Black interrupted in.

"And no one fell!" Miss Monopoly added.

"Dancers, I'm so impressed" Mr. Stone began. "Your level of professionalism, skill level and overall attention to corrections, focus and artistry is noteworthy. I am so pleased for all of you. Watching you over this last week, I've marveled at what a good job your teachers have done, and how much you each have improved just in this last week. Well done; I also am so proud of all of you, which leads me to my next piece of information. After much thinking and weighing out your work, I am happy to announce the following dancers who will be awarded a scholarship to study in our summer intensive this year.

Gina held her breath. It seemed like the room had become frozen in literally a second as everyone waited to hear who had been chosen.

"Congratulations Charlotte Tuddeldum."

"Lottie!" Gina hugged her friend standing next to her.

"Congratulations Boxer twins."

Ben and Bill Boxer were an unexpected choice. Gina took a moment to digest this, and the fact that this math equation meant only one more recipient was left.

"And congratulations Viola Barkus. We look forward to seeing the four of you this summer."

Mr. Stone finished, and everyone attempted to swirl around the lucky dancers. Gina had a smile on her face, but it hid her utter disappointment, shock, and huge, sad let down. She had not counted on the Boxer boys being in the mix of contenders, and had honestly felt like she had a strong chance of being one of the lucky ones. She had let herself believe this after her strong moment standing in for Viola. She felt betrayed somehow, and wanted desperately just to go home where she could cry. It felt so surreal.

I didn't get it.
I didn't get it.
I didn't get it.

"Gina" Lottie said softly.

"I'm so happy for you Lottie."

"Thanks, but I don't know what to say. You were robbed."

Gina felt tears welling up, and didn't want for anyone to see her lose her composure. She reached out and touched Lottie's arm, and knew she had to try to pretend to be happy for everyone else or look like a sore loser. What she desperately wanted was to discretely leave the stage area. Instead, she forced herself to linger, faking that she was alright. When she couldn't stand it anymore, she pulled herself out of the crowd to leave.

"Gina!"

Gina stopped at Rosalie's call. She had been standing off to the side, and had heard Mr. Stone's announcement.

"Gina, come over here."

Gina walked over to the back corner where Rosalie was standing, and fought off the big choking cry she knew was imminent.

"Gina, don't let this ruin your beautiful dancing tonight. You are so special, and deserve one of those scholarships."

Gina was unable to meet Rosalie's eyes, feeling that if she did, she would dissolve.

Gina felt Rosalie take her shoulders.

"Gina, look at me."

Gina looked up, and Rosalie took her face into her hands.

"I know what it's like to be good, and not chosen. It's happened to me so many times in this career, but if you have talent, and you work hard and have a good attitude, your time will come."

Gina was silent, not knowing what to say in reply.

"Besides, even though those boys are interesting dancers, you can dance circles around them, and everyone knows that. I bet they just want to encourage them to continue with their studies because they're boys, and the dance world always needs more men."

Yes, but they're going, and I'm not.

Gina nodded, too emotional, and not wanting to actually speak. She heard Rosalie's words, but they didn't matter in this moment.

"Your time will definitely come" Rosalie repeated.

"Thank you" Gina replied, eager to break away. On top of her disappointment, she was embarrassed by Rosalie's sympathy. It made her feel like a failure.

Gina stripped off her tutu as quickly as she could, and threw on her clothes. She snuck out of the dressing room, and scampered like a mouse hugging the wall through a back hallway to a side door of the audience. She went through, and found her parents waiting in the lobby.

"Gina! It was so beautiful!" Alana gushed making her way to her.

"Can we go home?"

"What's wrong?"

"Can we just go, please?"

"Gina, what happened?"

"I didn't get it. Lottie, Viola and the Boxer boys did. I wasn't chosen."

Gina saw Alana register what this meant, and she hugged Gina. Thomas had made his way to them, and was taken aback by sensing something was wrong. Gina saw him and Alana exchange looks that spoke without words. What should have been such a triumphant night was ending so badly.

As she was ushered out of the theater, Gina heard Jake shout out through the crowd.

"Gina!"

Gina pretended she didn't hear. She just didn't care.

The ride home was a blur. Gina knew her parents were trying to bolster her ego by telling her how well she had, in fact, danced, but the words fell all around her but not in her.

Walking in to the house was also a blur. Benny and Miss Bumble asked how the show went, but Gina only responded with the barest response hoping the babysitter would take the hint and go home.

She needed to be alone to process, and getting to her room was imperative. When at last she was alone, Gina laid on her bed and began to cry.

She cried because she felt like she had deserved this honor: she had impressed everyone with her own Dew performance in dress rehearsal, she had tirelessly done those boring and time consuming theraband exercises, she had taken all her corrections and applied them, and she had always, always been a good student.

She cried more because Lottie was going, and she wasn't. And lastly, she cried because she felt betrayed by her own hope.

She heard the phone ringing downstairs, and hoped that none of her friends were calling her. She didn't want to talk to anyone. When no one came to her door, she continued to lay and feel miserable.

A short while later, she heard the doorbell, and then soft voices downstairs.

Please don't let anyone have come over!

Gina's dread intensified as she heard a quiet knock on her door a few minutes later.

"Gina?"

Silence.

"Gina, it's your Dad."

"Dad, I really don't want to talk to anyone" she said through the door.

Gina heard the door open slowly, and saw Thomas walk and sit on the side of the bed.

"Dad, I just want to be alone."

"Gina" Thomas said softly, taking her shoulders and lifting her upright to face him.

"Dad don't!" Gina protested. "I don't want sympathy; it just makes it worse. And especially from you; you weren't going to let me go even if I had gotten one of the spots."

"You're wrong. I was going to let you go" he said softly.

Gina looked up when he said this last sentence.

"I *am* going to let you go" he said putting his hand on her tear streaked cheek.

"What?"

"I *am* going to let you go. Viola's downstairs with her parents and Mr. Stone."

Chapter Thirty-One

Lottie Tuddeldum sat impatiently in the lobby of the Sandrun Hotel. On this first day of classes in New York, she was waiting for the bus which would take them all to the studios at The National Ballet. She was occupied by watching the Boxers across the room, who were ridiculously trying to balance a spoon on the tips of their noses.

"Amazing" she said out loud. "They act so stupid. How did they ever get here?"

"Who?" Gina replied.

"Those twins. Look at them!"

Gina looked over and indeed saw them playing with a spoon, of all toys.

Gina laughed, and switched topics.

"Did you hear from Viv?"

"Yes, she's looking forward to being an assistant with the younger dancers in Miss Angelica's summer session at home."

"She'll be great at that" Gina replied.

"When does Viola arrive here in New York? Lottie asked back.

"Next week. Her musical theater intensive starts one week later than ours. She said she'd get in contact with us when she gets here."

"Charlotte Tuddeldum!"

Gina recognized the voice of Miss Monopoly, who, in an unknown and most unpleasant turn of events, had become a chaperone to this trip.

"Is that the way you're planning on wearing your hair on this first day?" she said, emerging from an elevator.

Lottie's hands instinctively ran a course across her unruly hair, tucking in tendrils which defied the many spurts of hairspray she had spritzed on them.

"I would suggest you run to your room and put in more pins. You still have fifteen minutes before the bus will be here, and I simply won't have our school represented by sloppiness."

Lottie groaned, and turned to Gina.

"If the bus comes, save me a seat."

"Okay" Gina replied. Looking at Lottie's hair, she giggled thinking "some things never change."

But some things do. Gina was so grateful to be sitting here in this moment, waiting for the ride to the first day of the summer intensive. She reached down to re-read a congratulatory card sent from Jake, and then, vividly went through all the surprising events that led here.

She had gone downstairs that night of the performance, and was startled by seeing Mr. Stone sitting with the others around her kitchen table. This scene was surreal, like it was an everyday common dinner party. She looked around at this unusual gathering: Alana, Mr. Stone, Viola, Miss Angelica and Miss Patricia, all looking at her.

"Gina come sit down" she heard Alana say.

"What's going on?"

"Gina" Viola began, "you're taking my spot."

"What?"

Gina listened to Viola tell her about the night she missed rehearsal. Viola had left rehearsal the night Gina had talked to her, bolstered by Gina's support. She became determined that she could no longer play a puppet to both her mothers' lost dreams. She had come home and asked Patricia to talk, but things got out of hand. Patricia didn't want to hear of Viola's alternate plans, especially with the performance looming. She had called Angelica over the next day so that they both could try to talk some sense into her. This is where it started to go bad. Viola tried to be honest about her feelings the afternoon of the dress rehearsal, but both moms wouldn't listen. Viola had become desperate, and began yelling. They in turn began yelling back. Viola had started crying and became hysterical, and though Patricia and Angelica tried to calm her down, she just got more and more agitated about continuing this charade, even if it was dress rehearsal night. She had told them she was planning on faking an injury, or that she would just refuse to go out on her music. Frantic to diffuse the situation, Miss Angelica had finally asked "What do you want Viola?"

Viola had then told them her true dreams of musical theater. She told them that from the bottom of her heart, she didn't want to hurt either of them, but from that same hidden place she ached for a different career than the one they wished for her. She spoke about the secret voice lessons she had been taking for a while, and then to demonstrate this endeavor, she began to sing. Alana and Patricia sat spellbound by the rich tones and melody that came from their daughter. She had a beautiful voice. What struck each of them deeper was the passion that radiated from Viola's skin as she sang. This emotion was so genuine, and so absent in her ballet dancing. It left no room for either of them not to consider this different choice. They began to cry seeing their daughter so engaged for the first time.

Seeing both her mom's crying had broken Viola's defensive dam, and she also began to weep. Angelica and Patricia hugged her, which made her cry even more. Because she was so shaky afterwards, they decided it was best to let Gina do the dress rehearsal until they could process through all of this. They had asked Viola if Gina should do the performance as well, but Viola had taken Gina's advice and stated that she felt she wanted to perform, if only as a last tribute to her two moms. They secretly were pleased, and held out a small glimmer of hope that perhaps she could still change her mind after dancing Dew Drop.

Gina had done the dress rehearsal, and everyone, including Mr. Stone had been very impressed. So much so, that she was one of the top dancers in the mix for consideration of a summer scholarship. Things changed though, when Viola showed up the next day of the performance. First, Lottie had surprised everyone with her tour de force performance. Then Viola arrived fresh with new motivation, and was filled with enthusiasm to perhaps wrap up her ballet story in one final performance. Because she had had such a breakthrough with her moms, and because it could potentially be her last time in a ballet, Viola poured every ounce of hope and anticipation for the future into her Dew Drop performance. Just as Gina had thought while watching her, she was suddenly stunning. She had been thankful for Gina's guidance about dancing this final time, but knew that though it had been thrilling, she was even more elated about the idea of launching fully into musical theater studies.

"So, Gina, I had already decided to support the boys, and then Lottie's performance earned her a spot. After Viola wowed me, I ultimately decided to give her the opportunity not knowing all the facts. Unfortunately, that bumped you out" Mr. Stone had said sitting at the kitchen table.

"But I hadn't changed my mind" Viola continued, "and Mr. Stone didn't know anything about what was going on. When we all left the theater tonight, I knew I had to make things right. I told them that the reason I had danced so well was because I was intending it to be my last, and that it had been wonderful. However, I didn't want to study at the National Ballet this summer, and that you should definitely have my spot."

Gina recalled that moment when Mr. Stone had broken in and stated that they would love to have Gina study in New York, and asked Gina if she would like to take Viola's place.

Gina had looked quickly at her Dad, who nodded "yes."

Gina had discovered a lot during that Nutcracker season. She discovered that her Dad did support her, even though he fought for what he thought was best for her. In the end, he let her chase her dream. She discovered that there might be things you don't know about people that shape the way they act, and if you reach out, they might become friends. And like the words Rosalie had said to her, she discovered that if you work hard, your time will come.

Sitting in the lobby waiting and dumbfounded that the Boxers were still playing with that spoon, Gina's time had indeed come.

"Gina, the bus is here!" Lottie said flying past her.

Grabbing her belongings, Gina's new adventure beckoned.

"Right behind you!"

Andrew Carroll has enjoyed an extensive background in the performing arts. This includes performing nationally and internationally for nine years as a soloist with the Pennsylvania Ballet Company in Philadelphia, and a principal with the Ohio Ballet prior to that. His repertoire included: Prince Siegfried in Swan Lake, The Cavalier in The Nutcracker (in a plum tunic no less), principal roles in the Balanchine ballets of Square Dance, Serenade, Allegro Brilliant, The Four Temperaments, Agon, Western Symphony and Symphony in C among others, as well as principal roles in the works of numerous contemporary choreographers. His career spanned performing throughout the United States, as well as appearing throughout South America, China and Europe.

He now is an Associate Professor of Dance in the School of Theatre and Dance, College of The Arts at The University of South Florida in Tampa. He has produced many videos on behalf of bullying, dating violence, suicide awareness and human sex-trafficking, is an international speaker and master ballet teacher, and is being certified to teach Dance to Parkinson's patients.

He still goes to the Nutcracker each year.

CPSIA information can be obtained
at www.ICGtesting.com
Printed in the USA
BVHW071312180719
553799BV00002B/137/P